Hollywood After The Psycho

Brittany Roth

ISBN: 979-8-9881300-4-8

Editor: Emi Janisch

Cover Designer: Brittany Roth

Formatter: Michael Davie, Grim House Publishing

For those who had questions and sought justice for Julie, this one's for you.
(Please don't hate me if you don't like it.)

Dear Reader

Dear Reader,

I don't particularly feel this book has any harsh triggers. If you read the first book, Hollywood Psycho: The Julie Simon Story, you will understand what I mean by that statement. However, I do not want to be the source of any unwanted feelings—it would completely shatter my heart— so I will say this story depicts a woman who was deeply hurt by the people she trusted the most and is on a journey to overcome that. There is discussion about the harassment she faced in the first book, talk about suicide and a mention of being raped. It does not detail the incident, but it is implied from Dalton's perspective and articulated from Julie's perspective.

Julie's story was never intended to continue, but with some questions left unanswered, her narrative lives on, and I hope it leaves your heart happy knowing her ending.

If you feel triggered in any way, below is a list of references. Thank you for loving Julie as much as I do. As always, feel free to reach out if you need someone to talk to.

TikTok & Instagram: BrittRoth_Author

Love,
Brittany Roth

Emergency Services:

911

National Domestic Violence Hotline (24/7):

(800) 799-7233

Text BEGIN to 88788

www.thehotline.org

National Sexual Assault Hotline (24/7):

(800) 656-4673

www.RAINN.org

988 Suicide and Crisis Lifeline (24/7):

988

Text 988

www.988lifeline.org

instagram.com/BrittRoth_Author

tiktok.com/@BrittRoth_Author

Chapter 1
Julie 2023

"I can't believe this is happening right now. You, sitting in front of me, in this beautiful home I know you've created. Wow! It's nice to see you again, Julie."

"Yeah, it's nice to see you too."

"It's been a long time."

"Thirty years!"

"I know, it's wild! I can't believe it's been so long already. How have you been?"

"I've been good, I guess. I can't complain."

"Well, I'm happy we get to meet again, even if it's for the reason it is, being the . . . . . . you know . . . anniversary and all."

"Me too. You know, you gave me some great news the last time we saw each other. Hopefully this time will be just as great."

"I guess I did, didn't I? Huh, maybe you and I meeting again is a good omen? So, should we just get right into it then? Or?"

"Sounds fine to me."

"Alright, well like you said, it's been thirty years. It's hard to imagine what that even means to you. Surely, those events still have to have some effect on your life. Hopefully not, but it is the thirtieth anniversary of what people refer to your case as: the Hollywood Psycho case. I guess I'll ask you the same question I asked you back then. What do you think about all of this?"

"Yeah, I remember you asking me that. Well, it's hard to say. I mean, it's been years of me *trying* to live a life I find to be meaningful. You know, something I find worth living. Something I find 'normal.' Whatever that is. It's just been me, and a lot of time trying to be okay with myself. That will always be what my life is: just trying to be okay with who I am and being aware of the constant worry I'll have when it comes to trusting people in my everyday life. No matter how hard I try to work on it and pretend it isn't there, it always will be."

"I can see how having a major traumatic experience would be a constant battle you face each day. I know it can't be easy. I also know my words might not seem like much, but looking at you and seeing such a huge difference from the last time we met, I'd never guess what you've been through in your life. You know, first losing your parents at such a young age, then your grandmother who raised you, and as we all know, everything that happened to you back in 1993. I guess what I'm trying to say is, you look wonderful, Julie, truly."

"Thank you."

"You're welcome. Now, if you don't mind me asking, what's happened since the last time you and I spoke?"

"Of course, I don't mind. Otherwise we wouldn't have anything to talk about now, would we?"

"I guess not. So, what's been going on in your life? What's new with Julie Simon?"

"Well, I obviously got released from being in the psych

ward, as you can see. It took them a few months to get every-thing in order for my release, but I'm here, and I'm living. After my release, the Kane's apologized to me, which was . . . nice, but I can't bring back their daughter, so I don't really know what to do with that. I don't feel like I deserve an apology from them either, because they were led to believe I did something so horrible to her. They were just doing what any loving parents would do. What I hope mine would have done if they were still alive. They were fighting for their child. I guess if I think about it, it's just nice to know that *they know* I didn't do it. It kind of gives me a bit of a calming sense from the person I was back then, who thought I was the one to do it, if that makes any sense. Just because everyone made me believe I did it, but I didn't. I don't know, I've just tried to move on from everything because that's all I can do. It's taken me years of therapy and working on myself to feel even half as happy and normal as I once was. When you go through something like I did, you're changed forever. There's really no amount of therapy that will ever fix how broken you are inside."

"I'm sorry, Julie."

"Don't be. I've had so many people feel sorry for me my entire life. I don't need you to be another one."

"Saying sorry seems to be a formality we've grown accustomed to, whether we actually mean it or not. I often think about you and when we spoke the last time. Your life seemed to drastically change after our interview. What happened right after I told you the news?"

"After Roxy was found and the note was read, they reopened the case to make sure it was actually *her* who was behind it all and was responsible for killing Morgan. They wanted to make sure they weren't possibly letting out a potential murderer. Which is why it took a while, but I mean,

I was content with the routine I was in. With the meds I was on, I really didn't even care what all of that could mean for me. I was so lost and so far gone into the delusion that I had actually done it. So when it was proven it wasn't in fact me, I kind of just took it for what it was. A second chance in a way. Truthfully though, I really didn't know what was going on with everything. It happened slowly, but fast. I was being talked to and questioned by the police and my lawyers, but I was so drugged up that that little part of my life is cut out of my memory. I just remember my sweet Jeffrey and Dawson were there to give me a hug as soon as I stepped into the beautiful sunlight as a free woman."

"I remember them always sitting behind you during the trial. They were always so adamant about you being innocent. "

"Yeah, they were the only ones who ever believed me. They were there from the beginning, from when I was brand new to Hollywood. They took me under their wings, and I fled. But when I needed them, they were right there, fighting for me. They took me back with open arms, no questions asked, and brought me home to their apartment because, obviously, mine was no longer my home. I owe them everything. I really don't know what I did to deserve such caring and loving friends. They had taken care of *everything* for me. They cleaned out my apartment and put everything in storage, just hoping for a miracle. Then that miracle happened, and I'll always be grateful for them. They've done more for me than anyone in my life, besides my grandmother, and even after I treated them so poorly. I would never help someone who treated me the way I treated them. I guess that just goes to show what kind of gentlemen they are. And yes, over the years, I think I've made it up to them. I mean, not entirely, because I don't think I'll *ever* be able to fully repay them, but every once in a while I think I do."

"Oh, so you've stayed in touch?"

"Yes, I see them all the time, actually. They're my family."

"That's really nice to hear, Jules. Or do you like to be called Julie now?"

"I'd like to say I go by Julie and left everything that came along with Jules behind, but there's still a part of me that can't quite let her go. The good parts. I mean, I mostly go by Julie because that's what I tell people my name is, but I'll answer to Jules when I hear it. It's not that often, though. But when I do occasionally get called that, I can't help but give a little smile out of respect for that person I used to be and for what she went through."

"I think I understand what you mean. There's a whole part of you that's defined by Jules. The way it made you feel back then, like you were living this dream life you'd always wanted. Then there's the bad. I get how you wouldn't want to have any of that brought up, but at the same time, can appreciate the good memories that come along with that name. Since then, have you been recognized? I mean, do people ever come up to you and ask if you are who you are? It was a pretty big case back then, your face was everywhere. Then the whole drama of you being innocent in the end put you back into the media."

"For a while, yeah. People would come up to me, mostly in the beginning, or scream at me from across the street. But when your mind is in such a fragile state after having your entire world thrown upside down and then right side up again, it can be a bit much. I tried to change the way I looked in hopes that no one would notice me, so I dyed my hair and wore different clothes. I even changed the way I did my makeup. It got to the point where I didn't even want to recognize my own reflection. Very rarely did people still recognize me after I did all of that, and I still didn't like it. I ended up staying inside for months, just so I could be left alone. I know it wasn't healthy, but I was used to being alone even though I was never *actually* alone. Then the phone started to ring constantly from reporters, agents, even some directors. They either wanted to tell my story, show my story, and a few even tried to cast me in roles. Can you believe it? I mean, having the phone ring off the hook for acting had been my dream since I was a little girl, but I was *done* with Hollywood. I was done with trying to live the life I once thought I wanted. That's when Jeffrey and Dawson helped me find a small little town to live in where no one knew my name. I also legally changed my last name, which helped—I don't think I mentioned that. I wanted to be a new person. I didn't want to be forever stuck as the person I was for that short period of time in my life. You know?"

"Yes, I completely understand. I'd do the same thing. You deserve to have privacy. So in this little town, what did you do after you moved there? And for the years leading up until now? Did you ever meet anyone?"

"I pretty much stuck to myself in the beginning. I was the new outsider in a small town, but people were friendly. I honestly don't think anyone knew who I was, or at least they were kind enough to not say anything. I never told them who I was either. I just said I was Julie and had moved there from Missouri. I pretty much stuck to myself for a little while until Jeffrey and Dawson started to visit all the time. They really helped me make some friends in town. We told everyone they were my best friends from back home, and by then, they had actually started dating each other. They became closer throughout my whole ordeal and I guess they realized they were attracted to one another. They've created such a beautiful life together. I'm actually the godmother to their daughter. She's absolutely perfect. She's beautiful, she's smart, and so talented. Anyways, I eventually got a job at the local library and helped out in the local theater, building sets."

"You didn't want to act?"

"I thought about it, but I was too scared someone would figure out who I was. It's a shame to have to let a lifelong dream completely go, especially because all these years later I know no one would have known who I was. Like I said earlier though, I was done with Hollywood, which meant I was done with acting."

"Out of these friends you've made, did you ever meet anyone who was *more* than just a friend? Like a romantic partner to share your life with?"

"I know you'd like for me to say yes, and well, yes, I did. I did find someone who makes me incredibly happy, and before you ask, I *did* tell him who I was. I also swore him to secrecy to not tell anyone. He's honored it so far, and we've had a pretty good life together."

"That's fantastic, Julie! I'm sure everyone will be happy to hear that. But I guess . . . here we go. I don't want to beat around the bush anymore. I think you kind of know what I'm going to be getting at here. Umm— . . ."

"Just ask it."

"Okay. Have you been in contact or at any point over the years, been contacted by . . . . . . umm . . . . or have seen in any way . . . . uhh . . . . . . "

"You can say his name."

"Okay, thank you. Have you talked to Dalton Blake since everything happened? Or have you heard from him?"

"Well, like I told you all those years ago, why would I let

him see me when he was one of the two people to frame me for murder?"

"So, you haven't? Do you ever think about him? Or about what could have been if things were different?"

"Do you want me to tell you the truth?"

"Have you not been?"

"No, I have. There's just this thing about Dalton."

"What about him?"

"He's irresistible."

"I remember you saying something like that the last time we spoke."

"Yeah, but he's not like a regular person. He *really* gets under your skin. So, I did what anyone in my position would do."

"And what's that?"

"I got even."

Chapter 2
Dalton 1997

As soon as I looked up and saw her shy, beautiful face, I knew she was the woman I was going to spend the rest of my life with. It kind of hit me all at once, those feelings I'd never felt before. A feeling like all of a sudden, everything made sense.

I've been with a lot of girls. Girls who were pretty. Girls who threw themselves at me. Girls who were really just good for that one night, which it never went further than anyways. Those girls were more of a way to get a quick release. They didn't do anything else for me other than feeling good for a short period of time. They never made me feel the way she did, because when I saw her, when I saw Julie, everything was different. *She* was different. It was like everything and everyone around me didn't matter anymore. Like the world I grew up in was a thing of the past, and now I was finally going to experience what it meant to live.

That's what she did to me. She made me realize what I wanted out of life. How I wanted to live a life I had never experienced. A closeness, a bond. The kind of love only two people who were truly meant to be could share with one another. The kind of love you can't live without and want to keep growing. I never really had that before, and she kind of didn't either.

There was an instant connection between the two of us. A connection I think we both knew would only come once in a lifetime. She didn't have anyone and wanted to be loved, and I was numb to a world I didn't care about. We were both looking to be saved, and we found each other in the worst possible way. We were meant for one another, there's no denying that.

Sitting in that booth with the girl of my dreams right next to me was unlike anything I'd ever experienced before. Shit, I felt like I was on top of the world, and that was all only within the first few seconds of meeting her. Then it all came crashing down when Roxy gave me the look. Within those mere seconds between meeting the woman of my dreams and seeing the look from one of my best friends, I knew everything I had immediately felt for Julie was either going to be the best thing in the world or the worst fucking hell of my life.

I think we all know how that turned out.

I mean, there she was, right at my fingertips. The girl I knew I wanted to be in my life as more than someone I'd just spend one night with. The perfect girl. *My* perfect girl. *My* Julie.

And I let her slip away.

Chapter 3
Julie 2023

"What? Even? What do you mean you got even?"

"I read in the paper how he'd been released. I can't even begin to explain to you how it felt when I read the headline, 'Money Talks. Pretty Boy Blake Gets Out of Murder.' A part of me felt angry that he could just go back to living his regular life, being who he was, while I would be stuck living in a self-inflicted prison sentence for the rest of mine. It wasn't fair. He ruined *everything* for me. My life would *never* be normal again.

My therapist at the time kept telling me my feelings of hatred were valid. That I *should* be angry after what they—*he*—did to me. And yet, I still couldn't help but wonder what our life together would have been like without all of the crap that happened back then. I couldn't help but wonder what it would look like if we could have been together. The two of us, raising a family and growing old with each other, dancing in the kitchen, just being happy and in love. Everything I had ever wanted, everything I wanted with him.

It wasn't that easy to imagine though, because what I went through would always come back into my thoughts—

always. It would always be there, looming over me with no way to forget it. It didn't seem fair, because it wasn't. Why should *I* have to live in a constant mess of not being able to trust a single soul, and not being able to have the experiences a young adult should have in their twenties, all while someone else was not facing the consequences of their actions?

I kept telling my therapist that I felt trapped in an endless cycle of not being able to move on, because once I would get one little step ahead and feel happy, something like that headline would come into my life and destroy any progress I had made.

Dalton Blake. He would forever be the trigger of my nightmares.

Even though I tried my hardest to forget him, he would always be there in this little, far off fantasy life I once thought could have been possible. Sometimes it also seemed like I was looking for him amongst the faces of the people I saw. There would be some days where I wouldn't think about what happened, but I would think about *him*. Then all of the thoughts I pushed down would come forward and I would think of how I still loved him.

That's who he would always be to me. Not Dalton Blake, who aided in framing me for murder, but *Dalton Blake*, the man I would *always* be in love with no matter how hard I tried not to be.

I don't know for certain, but I think it's because I'll always be living in that time. Even if I work at it, which I have, I won't *ever* get past that time in my life. I can physically see myself getting older, and I know that I'm getting older, but a piece of my mind will forever be trapped in 1993. The piece that's still there is in love with Dalton. So, it's like he was the last man I've ever loved, and in a way, he'll forever be the only man I'll ever truly love. I know it sounds ridiculous. I'm hearing it now, out loud, as I'm speaking to you, but . . . . that's who he is.

Then one day, I couldn't take it anymore and decided I needed to see him. I don't know if it was because I needed to see if it was true that he was out, like I had to see it with my own eyes, or if I just needed to see the face, in person, that I had thought about every single day. Whatever it was, I knew I couldn't let him *see me,* because I didn't know what I would do if we looked in each other's eyes one more time.

I went into a little bit of a stalker-type mode. I want to say this right now that I'm not proud of what I did, but it was all still fresh in my mind. I mean, four years—well, by then it was about six from the time I first met them—that's no time at all in the proximity of the lifespan I've lived so far. So I hid in my car, parked outside of his house for days. I wasn't quite sure if he was even there, but I waited. That's all I could do. I wasn't going to walk up and knock on his front door, I wasn't that far gone. I just waited and watched to see if I could catch a little glimpse. I was only going to allow myself to stay for a few days before I would ultimately decide if I was being completely stupid or not. It was almost like reverting back to being Jules, when I had worked so hard to leave her long in the past.

Then, as fate would have it, just as I was about to drive away, I glanced up at the house that changed a part of me forever one last time, and my heart sank.

Dalton was standing in the second story window, looking out onto the street before him, looking as though that was it. That was his life. Like he had nothing else to live for. His reputation was shot. It was more of a once upon a time kind of thing. Something that would only be in his memories. I couldn't imagine anyone wanting to hang out with him anymore. He really didn't have any friends other than Chad and Sebastian, if they were even still around after so many years. But there he stood, looking out, and I couldn't help but notice this look of sadness upon his face. I'd even say he looked depressed, like he knew he wouldn't amount to anything again. He wasn't *Dalton Blake* anymore, the bad boy everyone wanted. He was just Dalton Blake, someone people would eventually forget about.

As he stood in the window, aimlessly looking out at the cars parked on the street, my heart stopped. It almost didn't feel real seeing him after all that time had passed, but he was there, and he was *free*. My knuckles turned white as they gripped the steering wheel tightly, trying to steady myself from the uncontrollable shaking that had come over me from the mere sight of the man I knew I was still in love with. The man who would always have a special place in my heart, no matter how much I didn't want him to.

I sat there frozen in disbelief that after so many days of waiting, he was finally right there. It was as if in the moment I was about to give up, the universe showed me I still needed to hold on. He still had a part of me and it wasn't over between us. There would be something more, something greater, that was going to happen in our lives together. I just didn't know what.

After sitting there, lost in the thought of Dalton Blake and everything that went on between us, I didn't realize how long I had been stationed there until a car honked its horn, startling me back to reality. I looked back up to the window hoping to catch one more glimpse of him before speeding away, but he was gone.

My heart began beating rapidly, and my breathing grew erratic. I knew, deep down, I shouldn't have done what I did. I shouldn't have gone there. I was foolish to think I needed to see him one more time. But I let the piece of myself who I had worked so hard to erase, completely shatter the new woman I had built. Seeing him through my new eyes, my new identity, gave me the false feeling of closure I told myself I wanted, but in reality, seeing him was the only thing that would allow me to die happy.

I closed my eyes, rolled my shoulders back, and let the breath out I had been holding in, trying to shake off how I was feeling. I took another deep breath before putting my car into drive. As I began to open my eyes and slowly tapped the gas, I heard, "JULIE!"

I slammed the brakes, nearly hitting him. My body flew forward from the jolt and quickly back against the seat. My hands were still gripping the steering wheel tightly, as if somehow doing that would make was what about to inevitably happen disappear. I shifted my vision up, looking out the window and into the eyes that once fueled the love I had for him.

"Dalton," I whispered. As his name left my breath, I instantly knew I wasn't in the same place I thought I was. I was someplace I'd never been, feeling things I'd never felt. This new rush of feelings had me thinking only one thing: I had to get revenge.

Chapter 4
Dalton 1997

I never wanted to murder anyone. It was more of a ruse to keep Roxy happy, because when Roxy was happy she was fun to be around. When she wasn't, let's just say it was better for her to get her way. That wrath she would put upon you was something I wouldn't wish on my own worst enemy. I mean, look at what she did to Morgan. That's something you can't take back, and a piece of it will always stay with you, even if you didn't do it.

She'd always been like that too, willing to hurt someone because things weren't working out exactly how she wanted them to. Basically, to put it bluntly, Roxy Harrington was a fucking bitch and everyone knew it. She was born that way. Maybe if she grew up with parents who actually cared about her, things would be different. Who knows?! Maybe *she* would be different. But we all grew up like that. The only reason we were born was because our parents wanted to show off to their friends, to this weird, societal world we were born into. They had us, let the nannies raise us and then only wanted us around when they needed the perfect family image. We weren't their children to them. We were these little, tiny business opportunities only around to sell what they were trying to portray. The perfect fucking family.

No kid wants to grow up like that. I would have killed—well, I would have liked to have been told 'no' once in my life, or at least have been told I couldn't do something. My parents never said it to me and neither did my nannies, because they were scared shitless of my mother. I mean, she wasn't that bad—not to me anyway—but she looked down on my nannies because they were the "help."

They were more than that to me, though. *They* were the mother figures I longed for. The maternal love I needed. It was like we had a revolving door at my house because they were in and out faster than I could even learn their names sometimes. I will say, there was one exception: Genevieve. She was the only constant in my life. The only one who could put up with my mother for as long as she did, which wasn't very long—two years. But those two years were long enough to make an impression on me. It made me realize how I really only had myself in this world. If I was lucky enough, someone could come along and make me feel loved and I'd get to love them back. That happened twice in my life. First with Genevieve, and then with Julie. My *beautiful* Julie.

Chapter 5
Julie 2023

"Julie, what do you mean by revenge? What did you do? Did something happen with Dalton?"

"I had to get back at him. I know he wasn't fully responsible, or even the one with the idea, for everything that happened to me. He was just the only one alive who would be able to pay for it."

"Julie. I— . . . "

"Listen. He hurt me, and in a moment of vulnerability, when our eyes met outside of his house for the first time in years, it's like it finally clicked. He wasn't everything I idolized him to be. He was no better than *her*. Just a spoiled, rich kid who had nothing better to do with his life than to ruin someone else's. To ruin *mine*."

"But didn't you read the note? He was in love with you."

"I could never get myself to read it. Why would someone who was in love with me not do everything in their power to fight hard enough to protect me? Have you thought about that?"

"I have, and I guess you're right. We as people have the urge to protect the ones we love."

"Are you in a relationship?"

"Yes. My wife and I have been married for twenty-seven years now."

"I assume you're in love then? So, if someone was trying to frame your spouse for murder, what would you do? Sit back and let it happen? Or do whatever it took to stop that person?"

"Well, I'd do whatever it took. I love my wife."

"See?"

"Yes, I see your point. I just don't know if I would get revenge on them."

"Well, I had a *very* good teacher."

"Julie."

"Yes?"

"What did you do? I hope it wasn't anything bad."

"Well, after he stopped in front of my car, he asked me to come inside."

~

"Hi," he said.

"Hi."

"Why don't you come in?"

"Umm, I don't know if I should."

"Please, Julie." He looked at me longingly, like that night at the bonfire. It was like he wanted to tell me something, but I knew by then he wasn't going to tell me anything at all. He never had before, so why would he start now?

"Dalton, I don't think it would be a very good idea." My voice was shaky. I'll admit, he still made me nervous. The only difference now was the nervousness wasn't because he gave me butterflies that were rapidly flapping their wings inside of my stomach. I was now nervous because he was someone who let more than one bad thing happen to me. I was a victim facing my predator for the first time. "After everything that happened, I just don't think— . . . "

"Then why are you here?"

I stared at him, unable to move my mouth to form an answer. The seconds felt like minutes, running their course through an unparalleled time where I was only able to look into the eyes that had once made me fall weak in the knees. The eyes I had basically once lived and breathed for. He was everything I thought I wanted, but only because he was all I ever knew. Everything about him was a façade and every-thing *now* was a lie. *He* was a lie, and he needed to pay. I didn't know what I was going to do, but he was presenting me with the first, easy step to take. So, I took it.

"Okay. We can talk. I'll come inside."

My eyes wandered around the room, feeling as if I had walked back in time. Everything was still in its picture perfect place. The only things missing were Chad and Sebastian, smoking weed or snorting lines from the couch. That room was filled with so many memories. There was the first time they made me do ecstasy. Then the time Dalton tried to come up and kiss me like nothing ever happened after I caught him in bed with Roxy. A million memories. But out of all of the memories coming back to me, the one that stuck out the most was when he pulled me back into that very room to kiss me the night everything truly changed. The night I should have realized I wasn't safe. I was caught fighting an internal battle of what was once love and a newfound hatred.

My past feelings started to slowly rise up from the place I had buried them deep down inside. It was a part so deep, my therapist didn't even know about it. I had to actively try not to think about the bad things, but it wasn't easy. The good things though, those were never mentioned. I held onto them as a little secret for myself so I could relive them whenever I needed to go back. Being there with him, in that room, reliving those good moments, didn't bring back the happy like they usually did though. They came trudging back up on a mission to destroy the one who originally made them feel happy. This time those memories made me angry. They made me wonder what he could possibly say that would make what he did even remotely okay. He could say sorry and how he never wanted any of those things to happen to me, but those would be empty words I could never forgive.

And as if on cue, "I'm sorry, Julie."

There they were. The empty words.

The room suddenly stood still and the long pause held between us filled the air with a deafening silence, where we could almost hear each other's thoughts asking who should speak first. I had nothing to prove to him. My thoughts remained focused on the center of his forehead, where I wasn't able to read his expression. He knew he had to break it.

"I know saying sorry doesn't make up for anything that happened, or for what Roxy did to you—for what *I* did to you. But there's something I was too scared to say to you back then that I have to say to you now. I *have* to. Julie," he paused, like he was still too scared to even say them now. "I, I love you, and I'll always love you. I loved you from the first second I saw you, and I haven't stopped. I just had to tell you and I know you probably don't feel the same way. I don't know if you ever did, but I'm sorry. I'm *so* sorry. I love you, Julie."

I used to dream about him saying those words to me. I would melt into his arms and smile while saying them right back. Then the two of us would kiss with the burning desire of wanting each other's bodies, *needing* them to be so close that we were one. Now, my heart felt *nothing*. Not even one little pang of lust at hearing the words that once could've changed everything.

"I know there's nothing I could ever say, or do, to make it up to you. I'd be a fucking stupid man if I didn't tell you, and I'll die trying if you could just give me a chance. A chance to love you how you should be loved. How you should have *always* been loved. I've thought about you every single day and wondered what I would do if I ever got lucky enough to see you again. I never thought it would happen, but I'm sorry. God Julie, I'm so sorry."

I stood there, staring at the desperate man Dalton had become, on his knee's begging for my forgiveness. Yet, there wasn't a single part of me that felt sorry for him. I only felt rage. Hatred.

"What am I supposed to say, Dalton?" I waited for an answer, but he only gave me a look of defeat. The control he used to have over me, where if he would have said jump, I would have jumped until I couldn't jump anymore, was now gone. The giddiness that once turned me into a school girl with a crush had left, and I was able to finally stand my ground as a woman stronger than I ever thought I could be. "Do you even realize what you actually did to me?"

"Julie, I . . . . . . "

"Dalton, you framed me for murder. Not to mention you were a *huge* part of having me psychologically fucked up for *years*. I still am. You don't know what it's like to be in a place surrounded by other crazy people, feeling like you're losing not only your mind, but yourself. You *completely* destroyed my life. I'll admit, I did love you back then. I was actually madly in love with you. I would have given up my entire life to run away with you the second you asked, but you didn't. The way you led me on didn't even leave room for me to know, for a fact, that I even had a chance with you. Then I caught you in bed with her. So, what was I supposed to think? But you know the thing that sticks out most in my mind is you didn't stop her when you had every opportunity to. Now, all these years later, you're telling me how you're in love with me and are expecting this grand gesture to just erase what you did to me? How could you *possibly* think I'd ever still love you or ever even forgive you?"

I could tell he was trying to show empathy behind his eyes, while mine were burning a hole through his damaged soul.

"But you're here."

The beating in my chest pounded all the way up to my ears. I didn't know if I wanted to run out the front door or if I wanted to run into his arms. All I could do was take a deep breath in a moment of indecisiveness to calm myself. As I stood there, before the man I knew my heart would always love, no matter how many times I told myself I didn't, I had no idea what I was going to do. Then the pounding in my ears became overpowered by a single word screaming in my head:

. . . *Revenge.*

"I know I shouldn't have come, I . . . . . . "

"Then why did you?"

He made it so hard to talk to him. Not because the answers weren't easy, but because every time he spoke, my head was in the present, but my heart was in the past. "I was curious. I wanted to see you, not talk to you. I just wanted to see *you* without you seeing *me*. In a way, kind of like getting some closure," I told him. "I just wanted to see you one last time."

"Last time?"

"Dalton, come on. Do you really expect us to pick up where we left off? I mean, we didn't even leave off anywhere.

You slept with Roxy and then didn't stop her that night. You're kidding yourself if you think this could ever be anything."

"Julie."

"STOP saying my name."

"Then what am I supposed to call you?"

"I don't care. Just don't say my name. I can't— . . . "

"What? Stand knowing you still feel the same way towards me? That you still love me? And now know that I've always loved you?"

"Dalton," I said firmly.

"Here, let me get us something to drink and we can talk, or not talk, whatever your name is." He smiled. "Would that be okay?"

This would be it. I had to make a choice. I could pull all the good that was hidden deep down and forget everything that happened, or I could stand up for myself and become the strong woman I had worked so hard to become over the years. This would be my only opportunity to make a move and get him back for what they did to me. If I didn't do it then, I knew I never would. So that's what I chose.

Chapter 6
Dalton 1997

I never wanted to call her Jules. The only reason I ever did was because I didn't want Roxy to find out I was actually in love with her. Because, knowing Roxy, she would do more harm to Julie than what she was already planning on doing. Roxy was the type of person who always got her way. When she didn't, whatever was stopping her would be fair game for her to destroy. I mean, look what she did to Morgan who was just trying to help her. Since I knew not to cross Roxy, I knew she couldn't find out I had feelings for Julie because then *I* would be the thing getting in her way, and that wasn't a place I wanted to be.

My intentions were to stop her, Roxy, and I *was* going to stop her. I didn't want to let it get as far as it did, but then it did, and it was all because of me. It was my fault. I know it was my fault. I *admit* that it was my fault. It was my *goddamn fucking fault*.

Roxy was holding something over my head which made me feel trapped in her delusional, coked-up craziness. Thinking back on it now, it was fucking stupid and shouldn't have mattered in the end. What *should* have mattered, and *should* have been the most important thing, was protecting Julie, and I didn't do that. Now that's something I have to live with every day, knowing that I let the most amazing woman slip right through my fingertips because I wasn't man enough to do the one thing I know I was put on this Earth to do: protect her. I know she'll never forgive me, but if I ever get the chance to tell her I'm sorry, I want to let her know that I'll be making it up to her for the rest of my life, even though I know she probably wouldn't let me.

Around that time, Roxy went fucking nuts. She had been doing more coke than she had let on and Chad and Sebastian weren't keeping track of how much she was doing. They would just give it to her like candy, but they didn't care, because they were doing it too. They saw it as having "fun." I mean, they didn't have a care in the world or a job to clock in to. So of course their days were wasted away by getting high and sitting in front of my TV. Then, on top of the amount they were doing together, Roxy was probably taking some more shit we didn't even know about. Every time you saw the three of them, they were always getting messed up together. Sometimes they were so far gone they had no recollection of what day it was or how many days had passed. That's just how it was with them. They didn't care about anything, only Roxy did, but the only thing she cared about was herself.

For me, I'd only ever dabbled with ecstasy, and it was only ever on rare occasions, so I didn't really know what coke did or didn't do to them. Sometimes they would have a ton of energy and wanted to do anything and everything. Other times they just sat back on my couch wasting the days away. I don't know, maybe that was the pot. I like to be in control of what I feel and not have something interfering with that, but not her. Roxy liked to be out of control. She felt like the coke helped her act out on all of her little impulses she wouldn't do sober. It didn't make sense really, because she was the type of person who *would* do anything. Although she had bitchy behavior, she knew no one would stop her. I mean, she always seemed like nothing bothered her, or nothing ever would. I guess you can know someone practically your entire life and yet, not really know them at all. No one knows what goes on in someone else's mind. Roxy seemed like she was always having fun so you'd never suspect she was in a place where she would have wanted to kill someone. I mean, what gets a person to think that it's even okay to do that?

I know she was pissed because someone finally had the balls to stand up to her and not want to give in to her shit anymore. She hated that. So even though Morgan believed she was doing the right thing, to help a friend, it didn't end well, obviously.

God, I still can't fucking believe it. *I* let it happen. I let it *fucking* happen. I deserve to be where I am. I deserve every second of it. I let someone manipulate me, end a friend's life, and completely change the life of someone I care about. Someone I love.

The funny thing is, I never thought I was the type of person who could easily *be* manipulated because I was this man of power in a way. At least in our circle of acquaintances I was. I never had to pursue anyone. I was always the one being pursued because of how I carried myself. If anything, I was the one manipulating everyone else. But God, I should have stopped her. It's something I never stop thinking about. I don't know what made me so afraid. Afraid of her, I mean. I could care less if my family went down. My dad's an asshole and always has been. My mom would get over it. She'd divorce my dad and find someone else to foot the bill and put up with her bullshit. I would be a distant memory. Like some fallen rock star who everyone vaguely remembers and wouldn't care about anymore.

I never wanted to be in the spotlight anyway. I was just lucky enough to be born handsome and into a family who had some sort of social standing. I admit it now because when I look back on my life and how I've lived it, I used the girls who threw themselves at me as an escape from living under this scope of never being good enough for my father. They were a way to pass the time. To pass the nights, really. I can't complain about that because I *did* have a good time, but for very selfish reasons.

That's why Julie was different. When I met her, everything kind of became bright, like the light suddenly turned on and I now had a reason to be here. I had her.

She was so different than the girls I was usually with. She was smart, she was beautiful, and she was shy, standing next to the table when we first met. I'm not stupid, I know the effect I have on women. I won't deny it because it's something that's really benefitted me in the past. I could tell she liked me and upon looking at her beautiful face, with that smile that could light up a room, I fell in love. I'd never been before. But when I looked at her, I was struck by her beauty. Then I began breathing in her scent, and I was a gone man. I'd give everything up for her.

Then Roxy gave me the look, and everything I'd been feeling in the sixty seconds of meeting Julie sank to the pit of my stomach. I knew I had to do something before this perfect woman was taken from me and my life would change forever.

Chapter 7
Julie 2023

"Julie, should you be telling me this? We're on the record right now."

"I don't have anything to hide. Especially after what they did to me. I feel everything I did was . . . . just. So, I'll continue if that's okay."

"Okay. Yeah, a-a-alright. Keep going."

"When Dalton left the room, I knew that was going to be my only chance. I scrambled to pull the chloroform and rag out of my bag."

"Wait! You had chloroform on you? Why?"

"Like I said, I didn't plan to do anything, but that doesn't mean I didn't go prepared.

When he came back into the room, I was standing by the mantle, pretending to reminisce on the life I once lived with him, Roxy, and the guys.

~

"So how have Chad and Sebastian been? I haven't heard anything about them in a while."

"The last I heard, they both were sent to rehab. They did fine for a while after getting out, but Sebastian relapsed."

"You don't hang out with them anymore?"

"Well, I've been in prison for the past four years, so no."

"Oh, I just assumed you— . . . "

"Kept in touch? No, they were a part of a life I don't ever want to think about."

"Well, then maybe I should go."

"No, Ju— . . . . . . I mean, no. You're the *only* part of that life I want to think about."

"You're pretty confident with yourself, Dalton, thinking you'll ever have me."

I could hear his footsteps approaching from behind. I knew what he was trying to do. He was going to try to seduce me. He thought I was still the naïve, young girl who would once be there for his every beck and call. The young, naïve girl who still felt those butterflies anytime he spoke. But I wasn't that young, naïve girl anymore. I had worked *too hard* to leave that girl behind. Even though a little piece of her memory would always be there, that girl was long gone.

I felt his closeness, mere inches from my body, his warmth starting to raise the hair on my skin and I instantly knew it was my shot. I spun around, putting the soaked rag to his face. As his eyes began to roll back and his lids fell heavy, his body became limp and he melted into my arms.

Since I didn't have a plan and was solely acting on a whim, I didn't know what my next move was going to be. He was too heavy to drag upstairs, really, almost too heavy to drag anywhere, but I remembered there was a maid's quarters down the hall, off of the kitchen. It took me a while, but I was able to get him there and handcuff him to a chair.

From there, I kind of lost sight of what I was doing. Before I knew it, I was out of control.

~

"What do you mean by that? That you were out of control."

"Well, he woke up, and it was like I did too. Except he was groggy, with a look of panic in his eyes, and I felt alive, with determination in mine."

~

"What the fuck? Julie? JULIE? What are you doing?"

"Did you really think I was going to let you get away with it, Dalton? You fucking ruined my life," I said to him.

"What are you planning on doing, Julie?" He suddenly appeared so small to me now.

I was winging everything, every movement, every word. Like I've said a few times now, I didn't know what I was going to do, but somehow, the words came out of me. "I'm going to play a little game with you, like you all played with me."

"What the fuck does that mean, Julie?" he pleaded. "You know it wasn't me. It was her."

"Oh, but it was *very* much you, Dalton." I began walking towards him, this glimmer of revenge in my eyes. "You could have warned me at any point during those months. We even spent time alone together where you could have said some-thing, *anything*, but you didn't."

"Yeah, but I was trying to get to know you. I didn't want you to run off. I— . . . "

"You what?! Loved me?"

He looked at me, a sadness in his eyes. "I still do."

Silence filled the room.

"I'm sorry, Julie. I know I didn't do anything and I should have. Trust me. I beat myself up about it every day."

"Hmm, trust you? If I remember correctly, the last time you asked me to trust you, I took ecstasy and got raped. So why would I trust you now? Your words don't mean anything to me, Dalton. They're empty."

"And what did he say to that?"

"There wasn't much for him *to* say. He knew it was the truth."

"So, was that it? Did you let him go? I mean, that seems pretty powerful. The statement you made to him, that's a truth I'd never forget. I'd have to live with that forever. Please tell me you let him go, Julie. I don't know how I feel about this."

"Words, yes, can be a very powerful thing, but it's the actions that are the most memorable. I guess Roxy and I were more alike than I thought. I had never wanted to hurt anybody, and wasn't raised that way, but once I got that first little taste, it was hard to pull back."

"I'm feeling a bit uncomfortable, Julie. I don't know if we should continue."

"Come on. I know you want to know."

"I, uhh . . . . . . "

"It could be our little secret. *Off* the record."

Chapter 8
Dalton 1997

onestly, I never thought she'd go through with it. I kind of thought she was joking, or at least hoping she was. We all knew Roxy was crazy, wild even. Like I said, you really don't know someone no matter how well you think you do.

We'd known each other our entire lives because of our parents. If I had to name the person I could always rely on, it was her. If I had to name the person who had my back no matter what, it was her. She was my best friend, and I think I was hers too, only because she didn't see me as someone she could control or boss around like Chad or Sebastian. She saw me as her equal, or so I thought.

When I read in her note how she was in love with me, I was kind of floored. I never saw her like that and she didn't exactly show affection towards me in that way. So to find out how she felt was weird because it wasn't something I would have ever guessed.

Sure, we had slept together here and there throughout the years, but it never meant anything. She would sleep with

Chad and Sebastian too. To think of it, she never had a boyfriend. She was the type of girl who didn't want to be tied down, and I think guys were intimidated by that. She was Roxy Harrington. Her dad was a legend and she had made a name for herself around town. So, guys would sleep with her just to say they had. Exactly what the girls did with me.

I will say, in happier times, it was never a dull moment when you were with Roxy, when she was in a good mood that is. She always had these ideas that made our lives more fun. I mean being able to do anything and get away with anything gets old after a while, but somehow she made everything more exciting.

I have one vivid memory of her I'll never forget. We were thirteen and our parents were God knows where. It was 1980, so times were changing, we were entering a new era and everything kind of seemed like anything was possible. But everything feels like that at that age.

We had just smoked some pot when Roxy had the brilliant idea to sneak up to the Hollywood sign.

"Yeah, let's do it!" Chad said, his face lighting up with this sense of adventure. The kind only kids could get. So, we did. We went.

I had my driver take the four of us up there. We didn't tell him what we planned to do because he probably would have tried to stop us. Who knows, maybe not, seeing as he was on my parents' payroll. But I remember there was a thrill in what we were doing. We all felt it. The rush of knowing we could get caught, but also knowing it would be a mere slap on the wrist because our parents and their lawyers would make it all disappear. And that made it all the more exciting. I mean what could be more fun than hanging out with your best friends and getting yourselves into some trouble? We thought we were doing what normal kids did. Normal kids who had drivers and no parental supervision.

By the time we got there, it was dark and we could barely see. We didn't think to bring flashlights because why would kids who went on vacations to resorts all over the world think to bring a simple necessity on probably one of the only true adventures they had ever taken.

"Hurry up!" She called to us, her agitated tone already in place from us not following her lead. Chad and Sebastian had been shoving each other, joking how they were going to push one another down the mountain. "Stop messing around."

"Why are we here anyway?" Sebastian asked.

"I want to see our city from the top of the world."

"I don't think that's right, Rox," Chad laughed.

"Like you would know." Sebastian nudged him, causing him to stumble.

"Guys, come on." I pushed them both from behind and they stopped.

Roxy was the free spirit, Chad and Sebastian were the tag-a-longs, just there to be there, and I was the voice of reason, always getting them to calm down and follow whatever Roxy wanted us to do. It had always been like that, ever since I could remember. We kind of worshipped her in a way. She was always who she was, and never changed for anything or anyone. That's something to envy about her, I guess. She wouldn't let anyone manipulate her the way she manipulated us.

"Shut up and get over here," she yelled.

We got over to where she was standing and took in the view of our city. It was breathtaking. It was like seeing our world from the outside and realizing we were just a small piece of something much larger. But that's not what it was to

Roxy. I looked at her and saw the look of pride she had on her face. This look of, *this is mine*. That's when I knew we'd be friends forever. She was unlike anyone I had ever met in my thirteen years of life. She was someone who would go out and take what she wanted, and not just because of her bossiness, but because she was someone who would make something much larger of herself. She would be someone who could take over the world. I truly believed that about her. The world just wasn't aware of it yet. Then the drugs came, and the mean, bossy girl standing on the mountain top that night would now only be a memory of a girl who once was.

She changed after that. Her free spirit was always wild, but started to grow out of control. She was constantly trying to find more. More life? More love? I didn't know, but nothing seemed to keep her content.

When we met Morgan, I thought she was going to be a good influence on Roxy. She was raised similar to us, except her parents cared. You could tell she was, in a way, already put together. She wanted to help people and *not* use her father's name, unlike us who used our family names to get whatever we wanted.

I can only speak for myself, but I was happy when Morgan turned Roxy over to her parents and they forced her to go to rehab. Her being there gave us a little bit of a breather from who she had become. We never talked about it, but I know Chad and Sebastian, as much as they loved her, were happy she was gone too. They didn't do as many drugs while she was away. She was the enforcer and for a very short period of time, we could all just be still.

"I'M BACK!" Her voice carried through the foyer as she barged through my front door. "How much did you miss me?" The guys and I looked at each other in disbelief that she was out as soon as she was. Thirty days didn't seem long enough.

"Hey, Rox! We missed you!" Chad got up, embracing her in a hug I can only describe as forced, yet somehow meaningful.

"Of course you did!" She smiled, sitting next to Sebastian and nuzzling her head on his shoulder. "Now, let me have some."

"Should you be doing that, Roxy?"

She did the line without hesitation, then sat up sniffing a little before narrowing her eyes at me. "And how about you, Dalton?"

"What about me?"

"Did you miss me?"

I smiled to please her. "You know I did."

"Good." She leaned into Chad, squeezing his arm as if she were a lovesick puppy before bending forward to do another line.

She was never going to stop. Especially because someone was trying to make her.

When Morgan turned her in again, that's when she moved in with me, because she got kicked out of her parents' house.

I didn't want her there, I never wanted any of them there, but I couldn't say no. How could I turn her away when she was my best friend and she needed help? I know I didn't give her any, but maybe if I did, things would be different.

One day, when we were doing what we always did, hanging around my house, she casually mentioned what she wanted to do. "I've always wondered what it would be like to kill someone."

"What?" I turned towards her, caught off guard.

"I want to know what it would feel like."

"I imagine pretty shitty. I would feel bad. Guilty."

"No. Not how it would feel internally. I know it would be really fucked. I mean like, how it would feel physically. Like with my hands. How would it feel to take their life? Do you get what I mean?"

I thought about it for a second before answering, because it was a thought that had never crossed my mind. "Yeah, I think I get it. No emotions attached to it. Just doing it in the moment. I get it. I guess I wonder what that would feel like too." I really didn't want to know. I thought she was just being Roxy, and I knew she was high so I went along with what she was asking me because when Roxy was calm and high, she was nice. If I answered another way and she got mad, she would turn into another person.

"I want to kill Morgan."

As much as I wanted to, I couldn't turn away from her, not knowing if what she was saying was the truth, or some sort of bad trip she was on.

"What? Come on, Roxy." I decided she was joking. Everyone makes stupid jokes like that. I just didn't know, or think, that her joke was actually the truth. I played along, even when her face remained unchanged, knowing she was serious. And then I continued to play along when she later blackmailed me into helping her. I just never thought she'd actually go through with it. "Okay, how would you do it then?"

"I don't know yet. All I know is I want that bitch dead, and you're going to help me."

"No, I couldn't do it. Especially to someone I know and like. Morgan's nice."

"She's a fucking rat, Dalton. How can you fucking like her after what she did to me?" she snapped.

"She's a nice person, Roxy. That's all I meant. You know

she is. I couldn't kill her. It would have to be a stranger." I knew I upset her and had to try to make it right, *fast*. It was too late though. She had turned.

"You know . . . " She paused. "I know about the Blake family secret."

"What are you talking about?"

"Oh, nothing really, just the little secret that could destroy your entire family."

"Roxy?"

"I mean, one little slip to the media and I predict a little scandal on your hands, Dalton."

"I don't know what you're talking about."

"Oh, I know you know, Dalton. Just look at your dad. I wouldn't trust him from a mile away."

She was right. My dad was no saint, and he fucked up. There was more than one occasion where some of his patients were left botched and severely infected. He, under advisement from our family attorney, Freddie Steinberg, paid them off to keep their mouths shut and not sue. My dad didn't want to lose his practice, my mom didn't want to lose the money, and the family didn't want to lose our name or the power that came along with it in Beverly Hills. We were respected, or I should say, the act my parents put on was respected. My dad was who everyone went to for their little nips and tucks. At one point, he *was* really good, very detailed, subtle, but he started to let things slip when his vision started to go. He didn't want to lose his reputation as being the best, because his ego was far greater than any other important thing in his life. So, some surgeries started to not turn out how they normally would. Then, when his name came into question, well . . . . money talks.

I knew Roxy's mom was one of the ones infected by my dad's negligence. I just didn't know what she could be capable of with that knowledge. That's why I went along with it. I knew she wasn't all talk and no show. She was all talk and all show. I just didn't think she would be like that towards me. I clearly misjudged her. But that's what you get when you don't have direction and are expected to be a certain way.

Chapter 9
Julie 2023

Dalton didn't say anything. The tables were turned now, and he was the pawn in a game *I* was playing. Yes, the rules were being made up as we went along, but never the less, it was still fun. Well, at least I was finding out just how fun being on this side of the table could be.

I had Dalton locked in the room for days. I let him sit there alone, giving him time to think about his role in everything that happened, which gave me some sort of solace in my unplanned acts of revenge. I hadn't gone completely heartless though. Even though I was changed, I was still the girl who was raised with morals and values instilled in me by my grandmother. I would occasionally go in to give him food and water and let him use the bathroom. I would then immediately tie him back up afterwards. He never tried to fight me. He never questioned what I was doing. He just went along with it.

A couple of times, I went in there and talked to him. I told him about how terrified I was during that time. How I couldn't understand how people could do what they did to someone else. I told him how I lost my mind, and believed I actually murdered someone. I told him how hard it was to put in the work to tell my brain I hadn't actually done it.

"Do you know what it's like to completely lose who you are, Dalton? Where one day, you're a person filled with hopes and dreams and you're lucky enough to have someone special in your life who you're completely in love with. Then suddenly, before you know it, you're being told lies about yourself, and not just any lies. You're being told over and over again that you murdered someone, that *you* did it. Your prints were on the gun, when you've never even seen a gun in real life. Yet, these people, these strangers, mind you, continue to accuse you of murdering someone else. For whatever reason, you start to believe them and then you admit that it was you, but it wasn't you. And no matter how hard you're trying and fighting for yourself, you can't get them to believe the truth, *your* truth, so you think, *maybe I did murder someone*?"

He would sit there in silence, his head hung low, knowing he would never understand. Knowing that if he responded, nothing would change the situation he was in or the path he chose to go down. Maybe he even thought he could get hurt. I mean, he didn't know who I was anymore. He didn't know what I was capable of.

"If he said something, what would you have done? What would have happened to him?"

"Nothing really, but he didn't know that. I think he thought I could be capable of anything, and that's all I really wanted."

"What?"

"For him to be scared of me. I know it sounds stupid. I

just wanted to be his worst nightmare. I wanted him to live his life afraid to even look over his shoulder, kind of like me. They took the ability to trust away from me. Therapy has helped, but even with the people I do trust, sometimes I can't help but feel like they're trying to come at me or use me for something. I'm very wary of the people I let into my life, which is why my circle is so small. To live like I have to always keep an eye over my shoulder has, at times, put a strain on the quality of my life. I'm just fortunate to have people who love me and notice the toll it takes on my mind when those times come. They are patient with me because in those moments of doubt in the people I care about, it makes me have anxiety and a constant fear of not knowing what could happen next. I needed him to feel that same way. He needed to have the fear of knowing that *anytime, anywhere*, someone could be watching. Someone could *want* to hurt him.

His case wasn't as relevant then. It got brushed over rather quickly because no one cared about a rich kid getting out of a crime. But Dalton Blake wasn't just a regular 'rich kid.' He would always be known, and remembered, around Hollywood social scenes. People would probably whisper behind his back, but it wouldn't matter. He was still Dalton Blake. Girls would always throw themselves at him, hoping to spend one night with the now *notorious* Dalton Blake, an accomplice to murder. I'm sure that only added to his allure. And these girls would only hold him higher on the pedestal he was already on. He was now the *ultimate* desirable man, who could move on with his life just as easily as before."

"And you?"

"If someone found out who I was, I would get the same look of pity I got my entire life. I hate that look. So, I couldn't let it happen."

"Let what happen, exactly?"

"I couldn't let him continue to get the praise while I would forever be getting the shame. I needed to come up with an exact plan to get what I wanted out of this and I had to get creative. I had to make him want to do what Roxy did to herself.

Of course, it made me dig deep down to the place of anger and rage I never liked to think about, but that's kind of when it hit me. I would do *exactly* what they did to me, to *him*.

I would make him suffer. He would feel the highest of highs and the lowest of lows. I would make him want more, and then pull back at the right moment where he would be left feeling the loss of what could have been. It would be a full circle moment, and I knew the perfect place to start."

Chapter 10
Dalton 1997

"That's so fucking stupid, Roxy. We're not some dumb kids anymore."

"It sounds fun to me! I'm in!" Chad exclaimed.

"Yeah, me too!" Sebastian followed.

"Come on, Dalton. It's not like we're going to ruin her life or anything." She said it so casually, yet her devious smirk said otherwise. "We're just going to have a little bit of fun."

"Yeah, come on, Dalton. It'll be hilarious," Sebastian laughed.

"I don't want to do this and I don't think you guys should either."

"Dalton." Roxy pouted like a child. "Pretty please?"

How could I say no to that? Not because she was asking me, "nicely," to do something for her, but because if I didn't agree to her pleading, I'd be left on the side of her we all tried to avoid.

"Fine, I'll go, but only to make sure she's okay."

"Someone's in love," Chad cooed as I rolled my eyes and walked out of the room.

It was a stupid idea, childish really, and only went on to show the kind of person Roxy truly was. She didn't care about the feelings of others, or listening to what others had to say. When she thought something, she was the only one who was right and wouldn't even consider someone else's opinion being correct over hers. With this new idea she had come up with, and knowing what she was already wanting to do, adding this was just too much. I felt like I was being played a fool by my own friend. In hindsight, I was more fucking stupid than this idea because I didn't see what she could be capable of. If she could do such a thing to an innocent girl, then she would have no problem killing another.

I went, but didn't participate. Julie had already made an impact on me, so even though I didn't approve of what the three of them were going to do, which I tried to stop, I had to make sure she would be okay. I had to protect her, and I thought by being there, I *was*, but not to the scale I should have. Thinking back on it now, I feel like a complete idiot. No harm should have ever happened to Julie, and I will always regret that night and the nights after.

I was left out of the plans. My impression was that they were just going to tell her we were having a bonfire and they would interrogate her as a funny ruse. I didn't know Chad and Sebastian were going to kidnap her to bring her to the beach. When they threw her in the sand, it took everything in me to not run up to them and start throwing punches. I was so fucking angry. There was that thing though, looming over me —what *she* had over me—that made me refrain from beating the living shit out of them. I was too in my own head, thinking my family would go down if I didn't play along.

Then, Julie looked up, and our eyes met. I wanted to run through the flames and grab her in my arms. I wanted to kiss her like she'd never been kissed before. I wanted to grab her by the hand and get as far away from Roxy as possible so we could be together, just me and her. But I was afraid that if I even so much as took one step in her direction, Roxy would do something more to hurt her. To hurt Julie.

"Roxy, what are you planning on doing?"

"Why are you whispering?" she mocked.

"Roxy."

"Dalton." She stared at me, waiting to see my reaction, but when I didn't say anything else, she smiled. "Don't worry, it's gonna be fun!"

She had the guys drag Julie down to the water after Chad gave her a drink. I thought they were just being idiots, but when I saw the way they grabbed her by the arms, I knew I had to follow them down to the water's edge.

"What the fuck are you assholes doing?" I yelled.

"What? Come on, Dalton. We're just having a little bit of fun. She'll be fine." Chad laughed.

"Yeah, we only gave her one roofie," Sebastian added, as if it were the most normal thing to give to someone.

"No, she won't be fucking fine. Get her out of there!" I started to step into the oncoming water when Roxy grabbed me by the arm, pulling me back towards her. Her hands reached up to my face and she started kissing me. "This is fucking stupid. She's gonna drown," I yelled, pushing Roxy away from me and running into the water.

I reached her just in time and carried Julie back to the sand, laying her down gently to make sure she was alright. Her body was limp from fighting hard against the current and she was in and out of consciousness, but she was okay. She was alive.

I didn't say anything to any of them. Why would I have wanted to? I was so fucking pissed off. They had just almost taken her away from me. My Julie.

I picked up her soaking wet body and made the walk across the sand, putting her in my car as gently as I could. "Julie, stay with me. You're gonna be okay. I promise." She groaned as I buckled her in and proceeded to drive her home.

When we got to her place, I took off her wet clothes and put on the first things I saw, a pair of sweats I found on the floor and a t-shirt thrown on top of her bed. I tucked her in under the covers and then sat against her nightstand, watching her sleep, making sure nothing else would happen to her.

For hours, I stayed on the floor, watching her chest rise and fall, wondering what she would and wouldn't remember. I could hear the sounds of her breathing and kept thinking how nice it was to be there. How this was everything I've ever wanted. *She* was everything I'd ever wanted. I was finally caring for someone other than myself for the first time in my life, and there was no place I'd rather be than right there, on the floor in wet jeans, watching over the woman I was falling in love with. I didn't care if she woke up and wanted to know what I was doing there. I would profess the feelings I had for her. Julie was it for me.

As I sat there watching her sleep peacefully, looking even more beautiful from the light of the moon seeping in through her curtains, I couldn't help but let her know I would always be there for her. "I promise I won't let anything happen to you."

I jerked awake around 5:30, realizing I was still in her bedroom. I turned to check on her, only to find she was still sleeping soundly. I wanted to stay, but nerves came over me and I suddenly didn't want to have to explain what happened the night before. Especially because I didn't have anything to do with it. So, I made the decision to leave, but not before kissing her on the cheek and taking in one more look of the most beautiful girl I'd ever seen.

I regret it now. I regret it every fucking day. I should have stayed. I should have told her what Roxy did and what she was planning to do. I could have ended it all right there and saved Julie from the pain I caused her. I broke my promise to her, after I had only just made it.

Chapter 11
Julie 2023

"Since I can't obviously bring you to the beach, I figured this would have to suffice."

He sat still near the crackling flames, only flinching once to the popping embers. "Julie, I know what you're trying to do."

"Oh, I really don't think you do, Dalton. I also thought I told you to not say my name."

"I'm sorry."

"Empty, empty, empty." I tsked, shaking my head and walking over to his wet bar.

I watched him as I poured. He sat still, stoic. I knew he felt sorry. It wasn't an emotion he was trying to fake or even hide; he wore his heart on his sleeve. It was such a shame that it had to be this way, though. The way he tried to show me how much he cared and how he would do anything for me was something the old Julie would have surrendered to. I would have stopped all of the nonsense and accepted his apology, because I knew he wanted me. That just wasn't who I was anymore.

As I watched him, thinking about the actions the old me

would have taken, I suddenly had a realization that he could have been trying to distract me. He was the distraction before, and he was good at it. This time, he was trying to test me to see if I was strong enough to go through with what I wanted to be his outcome. He was once again manipulating me into something I didn't want to do, or even know I was doing. All I knew was that I *was* strong enough and *nothing* would get in my way of taking action on that repeated word in my head. . . . . . . Revenge.

"Do you remember that night? It's kind of silly to think someone who wasn't a child would do an initiation ceremony. I remember it pretty vividly. It felt like I was in a dream." I walked over to where he was sitting. "What was it that Chad said? Oh, yeah! Here, drink this." I shoved the glass I was holding towards him.

He took it and downed it without question.

"Thank you for making this so easy. Now, where was I? Oh, yes! The initiation. Do you remember staring at me from across the fire?" I paused, knowing he wouldn't answer. "You looked very sexy that night, Dalton, but I'm sure you and your ego already knew that." I smirked, amused with myself for stating a truth of his. "It's funny because I was so scared. I had basically been attacked in my own home and thrown in the trunk of a car. I had no idea where I was going, who had me, or whether or not I was going to live or die. When my body hit the sand and the blindfold was taken off, I remember feeling okay with everything that was happening. Want to know why?"

He sat in silence, only nodding his head slightly.

"Because when I looked up, I saw the one person who made me feel safe. The one person I knew wouldn't let anything bad happen to me. I saw *you,* Dalton. And I saw the way you looked at me. I had never felt the way you made me feel before. It felt like we were connected, like something was pulling us to be together. I don't know if you felt that too. Oh, wait. Of course you didn't, you almost let me drown." I started to chuckle, for the sheer insanity of what they had put me through. I mean, who does that to someone?

"I saved you, Julie," he whispered, his voice calm.

"What was that?"

"I saved you."

"Right, from *dying* that night. Are you expecting some sort of big celebration because you saved my life? Because I'm pretty sure if you would have done more that night, you could've saved the rest of it too." I reached up, pulling the blindfold from his eyes. "Bright, huh?"

Dalton tried to adjust to the glow of the flames, but remained in the same spot.

"What's wrong? Can't take the heat?"

He didn't answer. He was trying to go along with what I was doing to him. I knew it. I mean, why else would he be so calm? I wasn't that naïve girl anymore. I may not have been able to trust, but I sure as hell learned how to read people, and he was a man trying to do whatever he could to show his sorrow.

"Okay, I think that's enough of this. Get up, we're going to our next destination."

"And where would that be?" He stumbled as he started to rise.

"You okay there, Dalton? Be careful, a roofie can hit you out of nowhere." He flinched as I grabbed his arm. "Just relax. If anything, it'll make you feel better. Do you trust me?"

I lead him through the double doors and out to his back patio. "Julie, what are we . . . " he began to slur.

"Shh, don't worry. We're just going for a little swim."

We stood by the edge of his pool, his body starting to slump over. I was feeling pleased with myself that I was so ably reliving such a traumatic experience. I'm sure it's really hard for people to do, but I was finding it to be very enjoyable. As we continued to stand there, he started to fade even more, and I knew it was the perfect time to make him feel most of what I felt that night. So I pushed him in. I wanted him to see and feel, first hand, the fear I had. Real fear. True fear. A fear that only succumbing to letting it all go would be the choice you had to make to have it all seem okay, because it would make it end. I know my own boundaries. I know when you should and shouldn't do something. I know right from wrong. Although I knew what I was doing *was* wrong, it wasn't to the extent of what they had done to me. So I didn't leave him in there very long before pulling him out.

The weight from his wet clothing made it harder to drag him back to the maid's quarters. After taking his clothes off and tucking him into bed—see, I'm not completely heartless —I stood back and admired the body of the man I once would have melted for and given all of myself to.

That was all once upon a time though, back when I was in love with him and didn't know he was a part of a malicious plan to destroy my life. It's funny how karma comes back around and bites you in the ass. In my case though, *I* was the karma he never saw coming. I was reverse karma, getting my revenge for the bad that had been put upon me. I was revenge karma, out to get back what had been taken from me: . . . . . . my life.

Now I just had to make him sweat.

Chapter 12
Dalton 1997

B y the time I got home, I was the happiest I'd ever been in in my life. I had just left Julie's apartment, after watching her the whole night, feeling like the luckiest man in the world, thinking there was no way I was going to let anything happen to her. She was it. She had staked a place in my heart and that's where I wanted her to stay. But just as easily as those feelings of happiness Julie gave me arrived, they just as quickly started to fade when I walked in and saw who was sleeping on my couch. Roxy had her own room, as I had taken her in, but she would occasionally sleep in mine, except tonight, she was passed out with her head on Chad's lap and her feet on Sebastian's. I never let Chad or Sebastian sleep in my guest rooms, even though I had a few, because I never actually let them sleep over. If I would have allowed them too, they would have never left, and I liked to be alone.

"Where were you?" Roxy groaned.

"I'm going to sleep."

"Whatever," she said before nuzzling back onto Chad.

❧

When I woke up later that day, I couldn't stop thinking about Julie and how I couldn't wait to see her again. I had waited my entire life for the feeling she gave me, and now that I had it, I wasn't going to lose it, even though I was in a situation where if I didn't do anything, I could lose it forever.

I let a few days pass without giving her a call. I wanted to, I *really* wanted too, but didn't want it to get back to Roxy and have whatever she would do, happen. During those days of not being able to speak to her, or even see her, my heart ached in torture. Not that we'd ever really talked before, but I felt like we had somehow grown closer that night even though she was asleep and I could only look at her. The way her face would scrunch up and end with a smirk when I could tell she was dreaming, hopefully of me, told me more about her than words ever could. She felt safe to me, like no matter where I was in the world, if I was with her, I was home. So as a man who always got what he wanted, not being able to have her near me or breathe in her sweet scent or hear her soft voice, almost sent me over the edge. All I could think about was her and needing to be with her every single second. It was a new feeling for me, and a feeling I didn't want to go away.

Roxy was in my room watching some TV. "Hey, I know you mentioned you wanted me to take Jules on a date. I don't have anything to do so I'll take her on it tonight." I shrugged, trying to play it cool, like she was just going to be another girl to pass the night with.

"Oh, good! I told her the other day you were. I've been meaning to talk to you about it, I just keep forgetting."

"Okay, cool." I nodded, turning to walk out of the room so I didn't have to hide the smile my jaw was desperately clenching tight.

"Dalton!" She snapped her fingers like I was at her mercy. "Take her for a drive down Rodeo, then dinner at The

Chateau Marmont. You can even take her to The Griffith Observatory. People think it's so *Rebel Without a Cause*. Gag! But she'll get a kick out of it. She might actually think you like her." She rolled her eyes.

I nodded in agreement, but already knew where I was going to take her. I couldn't let Roxy control every aspect of my life. Besides, I *did* like Julie. I *cared* about Julie. This wasn't some pity date to keep her close to us. This was a *real* date I was lucky enough to take her on. My feelings for her were true and it was starting to get harder to hide them from Roxy. She definitely wasn't stupid and would probably start wondering why my usual serious demeanor had suddenly shifted. She was always attuned to that kind of stuff, noticing when we weren't really acting like ourselves. It wasn't often, so it would be more noticeable to her. Even Chad and Sebastian, who were doped up all the time, knew not to cross her. I just had to try to appear to be myself on the outside as much as I could, because I didn't want that date to just be a one-time thing. I was hoping to go on multiple dates with her so I could buy some time to figure everything out. Not only was I hoping to stop Roxy and her plan of killing Morgan and blaming Julie for it, I was going to use the time I was buying to spend more time with Julie. Just the two of us. Where we could continue to get to know each other, away from everyone. Away from what I was hoping wouldn't come.

"Okay, I'm gonna go call her then."

I turned to leave my bedroom, keeping my external attitude the same while internally I was on a natural high about to call the girl of my dreams and ask her to go on a date with me. Just as I was about to walk through the door, Roxy called me again. "Hey, Dalton?"

"Yeah?" I turned back to look at her.

"You can do anything except kiss her or fuck her. And I'll

know if you do. Okay, have fun!" She smiled, giving a look to prove she meant business before shooing me away in my own home.

I'm not the type of guy who gets nervous around beautiful women. It's always been easy to be around them. Especially when I've never had to do anything to get their attention. Like I've said, they've always thrown themselves at me. But when she opened the door and I saw her beautiful face, my whole world stopped. I'd never been in love with someone before, and yet somehow I knew I had fallen for her the second I saw her beautiful face.

My idea of a date, not that I'd ever really been on one, was making the girl I was with feel special. I'd only ever gone home with girls from the bar or club for the night, so I wanted it to feel romantic. I wanted it to be all about the two of us being together. I knew exactly where I wanted to take her. I knew exactly how I wanted to make her *feel*. I wanted her to feel like she could easily fall in love with me too. I mean, I could tell she thought I was good looking just by how shy she was around me. I just didn't know the extent as to how much she was in to me, whether it was just a crush or something more, like I was with her.

I did originally want to take her to the Griffith Observatory before Roxy told me to, but it wasn't just to look at the stars. I wanted to show her the Hollywood sign. It was my way of giving her her dream. I wanted to give her the world and if I wasn't so hung up on my father's reputation, I probably could have. Or at least I would have had the chance to.

When I turned her towards the landmark, my heart stopped. Seeing the look on her face of pure happiness and joy made me a goner. I don't think very many people get to witness seeing someone who doesn't have a bad bone in their body light up in the way she did for such a simple gesture of kindness shown towards her. It solidified what I had been feeling up until that point. Julie was it for me. Without her in my life, I didn't have a purpose. I thought I would just continue to live as I was. Living in a home bought by my father with bills paid by my father with no ambition to even think about the future. As much as my father despised me, I knew he wouldn't let his only child suffer in the sense of not living a well to do life.

Julie was the only girl who ever made me want more, not just for myself, but out of life. She made me start to think about the possibility of a future and wanting to make something of myself, and maybe start to actually pursue my passions. Then there was the way she made me want *her*. She had this pureness that made my heart soar where every thought that crossed my mind had her in it. The only way I can think to describe how she made me want to have a life where it would just be the two of us together is, *forever*.

As we drove through my city, the streets I had always been so familiar with somehow seemed different. The buildings were the same, the signs read the same words, I was just now seeing them through the eyes of a man in love and that's what made me realize how vastly different they looked from what I remembered. They weren't just streets I paid no attention to when I was that thirteen-year-old kid I used to be, back when my only ambition in the world was hanging out with my friends, looking for our next good time. These streets were now full of life, and possibilities. Things I never once imagined for myself, and it was all because of her. Watching her take in every moment from our car ride with the glimmer of hope and amazement in her eyes for something she wanted to obtain. She had a purpose. She had a dream and it was going to be me who would make it happen for her.

The Chateau Marmont, like Roxy had suggested, would have been fine. It just wasn't the right setting to be on a first date with the woman I couldn't stop wanting even if I tried. I wanted to give her the world, and in order to do that, I had to share a piece of mine with her. A piece that was solely mine and didn't have any remnants of Roxy, Chad or Sebastian lingering around. So, I took her to the one place I liked to go when I wanted to be alone. The one place I knew no one would say they saw me at. The one place I felt like I could be myself, The Polo Lounge.

The smile never faded from my face as we sat there talking throughout dinner. God, I kept looking at her and thinking *she's so fucking beautiful.* The way she would look at me with her green eyes, her pupils dilating every time our eyes made contact. She sent my heart on a rollercoaster of drum solo's simply by being in her presence. You'd think I was about to collapse from trying to hold all of the feelings of wanting to grab her and take her away to do things to her I'd never done with anyone else. Sure I fucked girls, but I'd never made love to one.

Then I would think about her reaction to what I had said in the car on the ride over, how she was *my girl.* The way her face lit up from the inside. Oh god, I'm the dumbest fucking bastard in the world to have not done it. She'd always be my girl. Even if I wasn't able to stop Roxy, which we all know I didn't, she would always be the girl I would think about and dream of being mine. She still is.

Getting through dinner was easy even though my nerves had me second guessing myself. Me, a confident man, never wary around a beautiful girl. She was different though. How could someone be as amazing as she was and not even know it? Her smile radiated from her face and the good in her heart was felt mere inches away. This caring, kind girl was more than what she thought she could be. She could make it as an actress solely on her beauty and the way she carried herself. Everybody would fall in love with her. I was secretly hoping she wouldn't make it because if she did, that would mean she would belong to the world when I only wanted her to belong to me.

After dinner, I knew I had to keep the night going. I didn't want to miss any chance I got to be with her by myself. I know it isn't what would be a typical spot for someone like me to take a girl to, but I loved being around people who didn't know who I was. I loved being around people who wouldn't question why I was there. So I took her to my favorite place of all, Venice Beach. I liked it so much because it was always filled with an array of people, artists, weirdos, muscle heads. It was a place I fit in because there wasn't one mold I had to fit into. Everyone was welcome. I did feel a little vulnerable taking her to places where I was exposing a side of me no one knew about. I tried to play it cool, but she was the only person to ever make me feel nervous. I had to keep reminding myself that all of this was normal. Feeling the way I did for someone was what you were supposed to feel. I should let it happen because I didn't want her to feel like I was some guy who was going to get what he wanted out of her and leave.

"Do you like comedy clubs?"

"I've never been."

"Julie, what've you been doing these past few months?"

She grabbed her arms, hugging herself in a timid embrace, shrugging with her sweet, shy smile. My eyes wouldn't have left hers if I didn't have to look at the road. My feelings for her only growing stronger as this beautiful woman sitting next me, so elegant and poised, had me wanting to become someone new in my own life. She was raised right, not like the girls you find running around L.A. She came from morals, from values, from someone who deeply cared. You could tell that that was all she knew. Something she took pride in in herself. I could see it in her. I could see it in her eyes. The funny thing is, she didn't even know just how perfect she was.

"I'm going to take you to one."

She beamed. Her smile, genuine and happy, knowing I wanted to spend more time with her, just the two of us. It was cute how I made her nervous, in a good way. It made me know, for certain, that she liked me. I mean it wasn't hard to tell. She kept that smile on her face while we continued to drive, and I wished more than anything to have been in her head, to know what she was thinking, what she was feeling. I knew I was the one who was on her mind. I just wanted to see how she saw me so I could match her image perfectly and be the only one on it for the rest of her life.

By the time we got to Venice, I could hardly hold myself back. I needed to be closer to her. I needed us to be more than what we were. I needed to feel her, whether it just be our hands intertwined or our faces so close I could feel the warmth of her breath on my skin. She was a good girl, and I wanted to honor that by taking my time with her. But there was this strong urge to be inside of her, making us the closest two can people can be. I refrained though from pulling my old Dalton moves because I respected her.

When I saw her in my jacket that nearly pushed me over the edge once more. I was used to getting what I wanted, when I wanted it, and although I wanted more, I couldn't wait another second. We sat down against a palm tree, Julie resting in my arms. The weight of her body feeling like it was the missing piece from my life that had suddenly appeared. Something came over me and I knew if I didn't kiss her right then, I would hate myself forever. That was probably the only smart decision I ever made.

Her lips touching mine was electrifying. I'd suddenly become a sap. I heard the marching band playing in the distance, the fireworks going off in the air. All the cliché's when it comes to the one you love. Sparks were flying. It took everything I had left to not bring her in closer and make love to her right there on the grass. Like I said, I wanted to respect her. Jumping her bones right there would have been coming from a part of the old Dalton. Whereas now, Julie had made every part of me new. I wanted to take my time with her, and fall in love with her properly.

I like to think of that night as the night that solidified everything for me. It was the night I knew I had to do something. I *had* to stop Roxy.

Chapter 13
Julie 2023

"While I was reveling in the beautiful predicament I found myself in, I started to think back on everything that had happened in my life. I'd be lying if I said I never thought about that time, but I'm only human and memories come up. So as much as I didn't want to, I started to wonder about Dalton and if he had ever genuinely tried to warn me in some way. The memory of our first date came to the forefront. Every second of that particular night was engrained in my memory because I was so in love with who I thought Dalton was, or the idea of who he was. But no matter how hard I tried to find something, or even pretend to think I did, he didn't reveal anything to me. He was a better actor than I was apparently. He made me believe he cared about me, although now I guess I know he actually did."

"See? Even though what he did to you was terrible, he had some redeeming qualities in him."

"Are you kidding? You didn't live what I went through. You didn't experience it first hand. None of what he did was redeeming."

"I think I'm just trying to find some good in this story,

Julie. Only because I'm afraid of where it's going. I've always wanted you to have the very best life and get whatever you wanted out of it, but if there is any violence against another, I personally cannot condone that."

"I was that way once too. Things change though when you have some of the best and worst things happening to you one after another. That's when you kind of lose sight on what's good or bad, right or wrong. You finally see that not all people are good. At least that's how it was for me. I was living in what appeared to be an ideal life with people who I thought were the perfect friends. I was in love with the perfect guy and they were all a part of the life I only ever dreamed possible. That life was perfect on paper, or in a script. What I couldn't see was that they were *never* going to lead me to my dream of becoming an actress. Because even though they were quintessentially in the right 'scene,' with Roxy promising she would tell her father about me, I was dreaming in color. She was never going to tell him about me because she never thought of anyone other than herself.

Look, I was twenty one, living on my own with no one I could turn to for advice and living in Los Angeles during one of the greatest times to be young and in Hollywood. I was also hanging out with the daughter of the biggest director of my generation. How could I not think life was anything other than perfect?

I know it probably sounds stupid to the people who have followed my story about how I willingly continued to hang out with people who nearly killed me. It's just no one will ever understand because they weren't experiencing what it felt like to be around these people. I said this many years ago, they were intoxicating. They were like a drug you couldn't get enough of. To be associated with them in *any* way was something to be proud of. It was like an instant badge of honor, making me popular by association. It also wasn't like I had randomly stumbled upon their group and started a conversation. They had *chosen* me, and to be chosen by them was something a lot of people could only ever wish for.

The way people looked at me when I was with them, especially girls when they saw me on Dalton's arm, was far different than how people saw me growing up. I had suddenly become popular which was something I never was. The night we went to The Viper Room made me realize I was something *more* than, when I had only ever felt less than my entire life. Imagine never being seen by anyone, and if you were, it was only ever from a look of pity because you were the poor little orphan girl. Then all of a sudden you were thrust into this *completely* different life, where you were suddenly being noticed, and those looks of pity turned into looks of envy. Being with them, being with *him*, made me feel like I had made it because I was being noticed in all of the right ways. I had become the person I'd always dreamed of becoming. I was becoming famous, through them, and the acting part would hopefully follow.

I like to think that that night would have still been as heightened in the sense of being full of adrenaline if I didn't have drugs in my system. I like to think that the sheer satisfaction of everyone's eyes on the girl on Dalton Blake's arm would have felt genuine, like a natural high from being gawked at in a way I looked at someone who *I* thought was beautiful. Sometimes that's a feeling I like to go back and revisit because for that very brief moment, I was more than who I was. I *was* one of them, and there was no better feeling in the world.

Then reality hits and it all comes crashing down. The dark memories, the *real* memories, come rushing back and I'm forced to face the harsh truth of getting raped. Then I start to think of the rage I have built up inside of me for him *allowing* me to lose the one piece of myself I truly valued most. A piece I only ever wanted to share with someone special . . . with him. That feeling creeps back in and I'm reminded of the little word that whispers continuously in the back in my mind, *revenge.*"

Chapter 14
Dalton 1997

I thought, 'This is it. This is the night I'm going to be able to show my girl off to the world. *My girl.* My *Incredible* girl.'

When I walked into the room and saw Julie standing in that little black dress, I just about lost it. I wanted to call off the night, throw her over my shoulder and bring her into my room where I could keep her there with me forever. She wasn't just beautiful, she was sexy and had no idea the impact on how she could make a man feel.

I had never been one to share things with people, even the ones I was closest too. But there was a part of me that wanted to tell Chad and Sebastian that there was more to Julie and me than they knew. I wanted to share this huge thing in my life with my "friends." It felt exciting to feel the way I did. The only thing was, is I didn't want it to get back to Roxy. At that time I didn't know she was in love with me and I sure as hell didn't want to be on her bad side because of the intentions she had. Her finding out I'd fallen for Julie would only send her off, and she wasn't the type of person to be happy for anyone, even a friend.

Roxy paraded in after Julie, plopping herself in-between the guys. I could hear them mumbling to each other, but my eyes couldn't leave Julie's. She had my full attention. Our connection was only broken when Sebastian called us over to where they were.

Splayed out in his hand were pills of ecstasy. This was one of those special occasions, so I took mine. Julie was hesitant, her body stiffened and I could tell she'd never taken one before. Of course she hadn't. I figured that if it was going to be her first time, I would let her know I would take care of her because I was going to. That was my plan. I wasn't going to let anything bad happen to her.

"Do you trust me?"

She was hesitant, but she still reached out for the pill and took it.

As we were heading out to begin our night of celebrating, I had to be closer to her without anyone seeing. I had to let her know how I felt.

Just before she walked out of the room, I pulled Julie back so I could look her in her beautiful eyes before the darkness of the night would make them harder to see. I needed to breathe her in and feel her lips on mine one last time before the little world we lived in would find out she was mine. I had to keep this little secret of ours just a little bit longer.

I remember being close to her, not wanting to move. I wanted to stay where we were, where it would always be just the two of us. Then I leaned in closer and whispered, and I'll never forget it because it really summed up how I felt about her, "You do incredible things to me, Julie."

She did. She was the one. But I let that night happen and I won't ever forgive myself for it.

∾

Having Julie on my arm brought out a sense of pride in me. I was showing the world that she was my girl even though she didn't even know it yet. I didn't need to announce it to everyone, but being seen with a beautiful woman on my arm would let our circle of hook ups and one night stands know I was a taken man. Roxy would think it was all part of the act I was supposed to be putting on, making Julie fall in love with me, but the feelings from both of us were real.

There's something about having the person you're in love with right there with you on display for everyone to see that makes your old life, before them, seem so pointless. Almost meaningless, really. It's a feeling of contentment, or feeling wholeness. I'm not sure how to quite explain that feeling. It's . . . it just felt like that's how my life was supposed to be. Whole and complete.

I saw the looks she was getting. I'm not blind. And yeah, I did start to grow jealous, but it also made her being there with me all the more, *real*. All the more, special. The girls were wondering who Julie was and how she was able to land me when they had been trying so hard for years to do that themselves. They would never figure it out though because they weren't anything like her. The guys were wondering who she was and how long it would last before they could maybe get a piece of my sloppy seconds. They didn't know that that wouldn't be the case. She was mine and only mine. No one else would ever have her.

My life's mission had become protecting Julie at all costs. I could see the ecstasy starting to kick in for her and immediately felt terrible for pressuring her into taking it. Roxy would have suspected something if I told Julie to refrain. I know it was a cheap trick asking her if she trusted me, but that was my way of letting her know everything would be okay because I wouldn't let anything bad happen to her.

That got fucked up, much like everything else in my life.

"Dalton, come here! I need your help!" Roxy tugged at my arm.

"I'm hanging with Julie. I'm good," I yelled over the music.

"No, come help me! It'll only take a second," she whined back.

"Fine." I left Julie with Sebastian, who had just brought over more drinks. I figured she would be safe with him because even though he was a dumb shit, he was harmless.

We walked past the line, not having to push our way through as the crowd parted ways for us. I could see girls eyeing me, wanting me. Before meeting Julie, the old Dalton would have grabbed the first one I saw and fucked her right there in the bathroom. It was different now, because I had her.

Roxy pushed me into a stall, locking it behind her.

"What do you need help with, Rox?"

"Are you having fun?"

"Yeah, I actually am. Is that why you brought me in here? To ask me if I'm having fun?"

"You look really sexy tonight, Dalton." She started to rub her hand against my arm.

I shrugged her off. "Okay, I'm gonna go back out there."

"No, wait!" She tugged at me again. "I need help."

I sighed, "With what?"

"With splitting these lines. You know I don't like doing it myself."

"Then why didn't you ask Chad or Sebastian? You know I don't touch this stuff."

"They're busy, and I missed you. I wanted to say hi." She smiled.

"Hi."

I grabbed the card from her and poured out what was in

the baggy on top of the metal toilet paper dispenser. I split the lines and watched her snort them, wanting her to hurry up so I could get back to Julie.

"Okay, are you good now?"

"Dalton, you're such a gentleman. Always taking care of me. I wonder why we've never tried to be a thing before. You know, like be together."

"We're too close for that."

"No, I mean we have good times sometimes. Why not have good times *all* the time?"

She was pressing herself against me, trying to get me to come on to her or fuck her in the stall. I pushed her away. "Come on Roxy. It's not like that between us. You're my best friend. It just . . . . I need a drink. I'm gonna head back out there."

I walked out with a sense of urgency to get back to her. The sea of women parted with their hands trying to grope me as I quickly rushed by. I began to search the crowd looking for my girl, but I couldn't find her anywhere. A sort of panic began to rise not knowing where she was. I was supposed to protect her and I wasn't doing that.

Then Sebastian walked over. "Hey man. Sup?"

"Yo, Seb, where's Julie?"

He shrugged. "She said she was tired, so Chad took her home."

"What?" I yelled.

"Yeah, dude, Julie's a rad chick, but she's a lightweight."

Anger was rising up inside of me as I flung past him. She had just been dancing, having what appeared to be the time of her life. There was no way she could have suddenly gotten tired and wanted to go home. Not without me. She would have been looking for me. She would have waited.

Something was off, and there was only one person who could have been behind it.

"Where is she?"

"Dalton! Don't be rude, say hi to Johnny." The conniving bitch smile she would give when she knew she'd won was plastered on her face.

"Where the fuck is she, Roxy?"

She turned towards Johnny, holding up her finger and mouthing, "One sec," before putting her attention back on to me. "I told Chad to take her somewhere. He was really eager to be the first one to *really* welcome her to our group." That fucking look was not leaving her face. "Don't worry though, Dalton. She's safe with Chad. She probably won't even *remember* the night." She winked and turned back to finish her conversation with Johnny.

Roxy Harrington lived up to her reputation of being a fucking bitch. I could have killed her in that second. I could have wrapped my hands around her neck and strangled the life out of her, but that wasn't me. There is the feeling of wanting to do something and then another of actually taking action. It wasn't who I was, or am. I've never been anything like her.

She took the one pure thing in my life and tainted it with her evil.

I stormed out of there, blind with fury that my Julie, my sweet Julie, was once again in the wrath of a fucking monster. And yet, it was still only the beginning if I couldn't get the balls to stop her.

I hailed a cab back to my place where I jumped into my car, racing towards her apartment. I didn't know what sort of situation I was going to find them in, but I knew I was going to rip Chad off of her and beat his ass for even attempting to do something I knew she didn't want to do. At least, not with him.

I left my car in the middle of the street and ran straight to her door. I turned the handle trying to open it, but it was locked. I began knocking, then banging on her door calling out her name. "Julie! Julie! Are you in there?" There was no answer. "Fuck!"

I ran back outside in a panic, looking up and down the street for Chad's car. It wasn't anywhere in sight. He was a dumb fuck, but I knew he wouldn't be that stupid to take her back to her own place. "Shit!" I got back into my car and started to drive around to the spots I knew Chad frequented. Again, his stupid, fucking car was nowhere in sight.

I've never felt so helpless than I did or as upset with myself as I was then. I let her out of my sight knowing Roxy was out of control. She needed to be stopped before she went through with killing Morgan. She needed to be stopped before she completely ruined Julie's life.

Chapter 15
Julie 2023

"Julie, you clearly still loved him. Wasn't what you did enough? I mean, I know what he did to you was unforgivable, but you both *loved* each other."

"Well, it's too late to go back now. What's done is done, and like I said, I'll always love Dalton, but it's not the same kind of love that it was back then. Now it's just a type of love formed around an idea of a man I used to be in love with. Sometimes it almost feels like he was a figment of my imagination because I was more invested in him than he was in me. I imagined a life with him, a happy life, which I was never able to live out. It was all something I just made up. Yes, he was a real person who I had very strong feelings for, but at the same time, those feelings got trapped in the idea of him before they could ever live out their truth.

I gave him a few days alone to think about things, to think about me. I felt bad for what I did so I let him be free in the room, but made sure all of the windows and doors were secure even though I knew he wouldn't try to escape. I would bring him food and water, only opening the door just enough to be able to slide the tray in before shutting it again. I wasn't ready to face him. I felt ashamed at myself for the way I was acting, but I also felt this sense of power knowing I was the one in control of what was happening. For the first time in my life, I wasn't the person people easily took advantage of, I was the one they didn't know was coming."

When I finally went to see him, I brought a bottle of champagne in a sort of effort to appease the situation.

"What's that for?"

"I thought we could have some, and talk."

"Talk?"

"Yeah. Talk."

"About what?"

"I wanted to apologize for the other day, Dalton. I kind of got carried away."

He rolled his eyes, smirking in a playful way.

"What?" I asked, unable to contain the smile he put on my face, and also unsure of why he seemed so at ease for what some would consider being very unusual circumstances.

"You know," he started, completely relaxed as if us being together were an everyday thing, like all of our history had never happened.

"What?"

He shook his head. "Never mind. You probably don't want to hear it."

"No, please. Tell me," I said, walking over to the night-stand before sitting on the edge of the bed and pouring each of us a glass.

"You're," he breathed out. "Still the most beautiful woman I've ever seen."

"Dalton."

"I mean it. Truthfully. I know I fucked up. I know I should have done whatever I could have to protect you. I just . . . . . . "

Again, I didn't know what to do. There was a part of me that could have easily let everything go and forgive him, but that would only make things more complicated. It would be taking the easy way out of an opportunity that was beautifully presented in front of me.

"Hey, do you remember that night we spent together out on the beach? Just the two of us?"

"I think about that night all the time." He looked at me longingly, his smile fading.

"What was your favorite part about it?" I nervously took a sip of champagne, eager to hear his answer. That night had meant so much to me. It was the night I knew we were truly meant for one another. He showed me his tender side, revealing what I know he'd never told anyone else. It was the night I knew he felt the same towards me even though it would take him years to finally admit. That night was where I felt like we were just two people in a world where we could be ourselves and not have to fit in anywhere else because we were fitting in together.

"Honestly?"

I nodded, wanting to know.

"Just lying there, hearing the sound of crashing waves with you in my arms. Everything about that night was perfect. That's the night I knew I didn't just love you. I was *in love* with you, Julie."

"Dalton."

"No, let me finish. I've never been in love with anyone before. You were and still are the only girl for me."

"Dalton, stop." The mood had suddenly shifted. I didn't want to hear him tell me how he felt about me. Everything was different now, or at least I had tried my hardest to make it different.

"I won't," he paused. "I'll never stop telling you because I'll never stop loving you. I *know* I fucked up. God dammit, I *fucking* know. And I know you'll never forgive me, which is why I'm enduring whatever this shit is because it means I get to spend time with you before you end what you're doing and we never see each other again. I would spend the rest of my life locked in this room if it means you'll be here with me."

I stood up, grabbing the bottle of champagne, not wanting to hear anymore. He had to stop, and I had to stop him because the words coming from his mouth were disrupting the feelings I fought so hard to push down. They had started to make me weak when I wasn't weak anymore. I had been for a long time, but I made myself stronger when I realized I was the only one who could control how I felt. I made myself resist him because I was also the only one who could protect myself. I lifted the bottle high above my head forcing all of the anger I was feeling with it as I threw it to the ground, watching it shatter to a million pieces. "I TOLD YOU TO STOP." I turned, running out of the room and slamming the door behind me.

I wasn't going to let him manipulate me again. Not this time. I had worked too hard to let everything be destroyed by a smoothly formulated expression of how he felt. He was calculated, but I was a woman out for revenge.

That night, when I prepared his food, I gave him another roofie. I know it wasn't something I should have done, but I wasn't the nice, innocent girl I used to be. I was a woman scorned, who wouldn't let anyone hurt me ever again.

～

"Why aren't you saying anything?"

"I don't really have anything *to* say. I get where you're coming from in doing what you did, I just don't know if I would have done it. I mean, I *know* I wouldn't have. There's a part of me though, maybe because I've been invested in your case since the beginning, that as much as I'm afraid to know the rest of your story, I feel like I *need* to know what happened."

"Well, since he obviously just fell asleep, I was able to be at peace with my thoughts knowing if I made any noise he wouldn't wake up. Truthfully, I had been put through so much pain, and frankly torture around that time, to finally be able to get some sort of redemption for myself felt therapeutic. Again, the lack of a plan led me to acting out on impulse instead of thoroughly thinking an idea through. But I thought, what better way for him to wake up then to wake up confused and frightened like I did.

I went into the room and destroyed it. Knocking over chairs. Artwork on the walls. Anything that had a specific place was thrown to the ground and some things were even got broken. It had always bothered me how his house was picture perfect. The unlived in aspect of it made it seem fake, just like him. It was a mask as to who he truly was."

"Then who was he?"

"He was a monster. A monster I was drawn to who continuously let these things happen to me. So, I had to make his home match who he was. I had to turn his picture-perfect life that couldn't get messed up into something that could get ruined, like mine.

Surely, he would wake up confused, like I did. *Especially* with the little added detail *I* would never forget about. When I allow myself to look back on all of it, that night specifically, I should have woken up, literally and figuratively, and realize I wasn't with the right people. I thought these 'friends' who had everything, who were accepting of a 'no body' outsider, were going to be what I had always been to people. I thought they would be what I had always been taught by my grandmother to be . . . kind. But they weren't. They couldn't even pretend to be. They were the epitome of what evil is. They were evil to their core, and I had myself caught up in it."

"You don't have to look at me like that. You know I hate it."

"I'm sorry Julie."

"Don't be. Just don't do it again.

I wanted to be there when he woke up to see the reaction on his face. I wanted to see the confusion, the panic, but I needed time away from him and he needed to simmer from the not knowing of what happened.

"I want to talk."

"Yeah, I think we . . ."

"No, *I* want to talk and I want *you* to listen."

He shut his mouth, nodding silently, giving me the allowance to speak.

"There was a time where having you all to myself would have been the biggest dream come true. *Bigger* than anything else. I was *madly* in love with you, Dalton, and I know you know that. But you have *no idea* the pain you've caused me. Not just because of the betrayal, but because I foolishly believed that you and I could have been something. We could have had something real. But you'll never know that kind of hurt. The hurt from someone you *so* desperately loved. I don't let many people in because I tend to lose them and I should have known then that I was going to lose you too. I just never imagined it was going to happen in the way that it did. You, Dalton, are one of two people in my life who I *truly* hate. You may come off as this somber man whose 'sorry' for his mistakes, but to the depths of your soul you are *not* a good person, Dalton. I don't think you ever were. And that's something *you* have to live with. Do you even realize that because of *you*, a beautiful young woman, who had all the potential in the world, is no longer alive? I mean, forget about me and my life, I still have mine to live even if it's full of anger and not being able to trust anyone. Hers is gone. And *you* took it away from her. You could have stopped Roxy. You could have saved me. You could have saved Morgan. But you didn't do anything. Not one goddamn thing."

Dalton continued to sit there in silence, his head hung low. He didn't have the courage to look me in the eyes at the trial and he didn't have the courage to look me in the eyes now. He murdered someone. I never realized it until I spoke those words out loud. He *murdered* someone. Here I was stuck in the pain that was inflicted on me, in how my innocence had been stripped away and my mind would never be the same again. He took that away from me, and in a way, it was worse than Roxy being the mastermind behind it all. Even though her hand was the one to actually do it, he had all the power to have stopped it. He could have stopped her. Instead, he let someone die. The blood was on *his* hands.

Although I had dreamt and fantasized about him, even after the fact, realizing who he actually was made all of that go away. He was a murderer. *The* murderer. It almost made me feel bad for Roxy.

～

"Wait, what? How could you feel bad for her?"

"I still hate her. I always will. I'm pretty sure she was mentally ill as well. You'd have to be to want to do what she did. But realizing that Dalton was the true murderer made Roxy seem all the more sad. Yes, she was a bitch, but she was a bitch with a problem and couldn't accept help, even though she had access to all the help in the world. She was sad and her only solution was to lose herself in drugs which made her do things out of her sound mind.

She's a tragic story. She didn't even have the chance to hit rock bottom and change her life around. She just hit rock bottom by taking the easy way out, which is actually the hardest way if you ask me.

I'm never going to be the girl I once was. It's easy to say that there might be remnants of her, but that's not true. Any glimpse of my old self was left in 1993 and there's no sign of her anywhere. She's gone forever, just like Morgan.

Now that I had this opportunity in my hands to do something in reference to not being able to do anything back then, I couldn't let myself pass it up. My hope was to break him. I wanted to shatter whatever existence he had left and feel like he couldn't go on living with himself. He needed to feel like there was nothing else to live for. Not even me."

Chapter 16
Dalton 1997

I drove around hoping for a miracle, even though I knew what was happening. I underestimated Roxy and my ability to keep things hidden from her. I thought I was being myself, playing it cool, not being obvious at all. If anything, I was being subtle. But she was smarter than me, at least two steps ahead in her plan, and I didn't see it. She figured it all out and was trying to show her dominance against me. How she wasn't going to let anything stop her from doing what she wanted. I may have acted as if I didn't care, but I'm not stupid either, or maybe I was. I knew what she was doing. The rage inside of me was like lighting, flashing anytime a mental image of Chad being with my Julie tore through my mind. I never wanted to kill anyone, but for a moment, I thought maybe I could.

It took me a while to convince myself that there was no use driving aimlessly around hoping to find them. Driving around was making it worse. So I decided to go back to my house to wait it out, in my place of calmness where I could think, and hopefully figure out what to do.

As I pulled into my driveway, Chad's car was parked

where he usually left it. The anxious rage fueled me once again, and all I could see was red.

I don't remember turning my car off or walking into my house. I was in a blind fury as I stormed in, heading straight to my living room and sucker punching Chad in the face.

"What the fuck, Dalton?" he yelled, clutching his left eye in his hands.

"WHY DID YOU FUCKING DO IT?"

Sebastian got up from the sunken in couch cushion and came up behind me, trying to hold me back from taking another swing at Chad.

"What? I was warming her up for you man."

"Guys! Guys, please!" Roxy started, looking pleased with herself. "Why do you even care so much, Dalton?"

"GET THE FUCK OUT OF MY HOUSE. ALL OF YOU. NOW."

"Jeez, what the fuck crawled up his butt?" Sebastian questioned.

I didn't stay to see them leave. I went straight to my bedroom, slamming the door behind me.

As I paced around my bed, walking back and forth in half circles, my rage kept building. I had to get it out before I fucking exploded. I was yelling, screaming, and punching the pillows on my bed all while picturing they were Chad's smug, prick-like face. There was a huge part of me that wanted to tell Roxy off, to end whatever our fucked up friendship had turned into, but every time I thought of the right thing to say, my Father's image would come to mind. That festering sense of guilt would get stuck in my throat which only fueled my rage even more. It was fucking frustrating being torn between him and the woman I was in love with. Then there was the fucking puppet master ready to destroy either one of them at the snap of her fingers. The ball was always in her court and I felt like there was no way out. I was trapped in this fucked up situation that would leave me destroyed on both ends. However, it was all up to me. Even though my father was a fucking asshole, I had to save him. Maybe I could save both of them, leaving me to be the one to get burned in the end. I just couldn't figure out how to do it. How to end it.

Chapter 17
Julie 2023

The idea came to me as I was drifting off to sleep. It jolted me awake, like a surge of energy rushing through my body. Excitement for life had once again returned to me as the idea kept unraveling in my mind. I knew what I was going to do with Dalton. I knew how I was going to get the revenge I had been winging for the past week.

I burst into the room, causing the door to make a dent into the wall behind it. Dalton sat up in a panic. "What the fuck?"

Without saying a word, I untied him from the bedside table and began to pull him behind me to my car. I shoved him into the front seat, buckling his seatbelt, knowing I was in control of what was about to happen. A somber tension filled the drive as his unknowing silence gave way to the devious plan my mind was conjuring up. There we were, just the two of us driving in the middle of the night, heading to the *one* destination I promised myself I would never return to. However, for what I wanted to do, it felt right to end it for him in the same place he ended it all for me.

I was ravenous in joy at the idea I had come up with. I drove with a smile on my face the entire way, knowing this was it. This was going to be the moment where I could live the rest of my life with peace of mind, knowing I had done it. I had made him pay.

My blissful silence was broken when he spoke, pulling me out of the satisfaction this was going to give me. "Julie? What are we doing here?" Panic was hiding in the undertones of his voice.

A smile filled my face as I turned towards him. "You'll see."

The gravel beneath the tires crunched as we slowed to a stop with a wave of vibrancy coming over me as I put my car in park and took the key out of the ignition. I felt proud of myself for thinking up such a plan. I had always been shy ever since I was a little girl, so it was kind of funny that the one thing I was so passionate about in life was to be on stage where you most definitely couldn't be shy. A new sense of self, a new me, a new Julie was what I thought the pride felt like. An outgoing Julie. A Julie who wouldn't let someone walk all over her like she had let in the past.

I stepped out of the car, taking in the crisp air of a cool night, and breathing deeply in, filling my lungs with the energy of what I was hoping would happen.

Each step towards his side of the car felt like the universe was giving me the strength to get this done. To get the ultimate revenge. The ultimate payback.

As I reached his door, about to grab the handle, I paused as I took a quick glance through the window. For a spilt second, I saw the man I fell in love with all those years ago trapped behind the eyes of a stranger. He was trying to call me back to him, trying to get me to stop, but he didn't say a word, just like he didn't say anything back then.

"Come on." I reached for the rope binding his wrists together.

"Julie, I don't want— . . . "

"Shh, it's okay. We need to be here."

"Why?"

I whipped around to face him. "Because it'll be fun." I smiled.

"This isn't like you, Julie."

"And how do you know that, Dalton?"

"Because I know you."

My eyes narrowed. "That's funny. I don't think you know me at all."

"Julie . . . . . . "

"I thought I told you to stop saying my name. Tsk, tsk, tsk. Dalton, you'll never be the man I— . . . "

"Listen," he interrupted, stopping our footsteps. "I know what I did was shitty, and I don't expect you to ever forgive me, but I *do* know you, and you're not like this. You're not like, *her*."

"Okay, Mr. Know-it-all, how am I then?"

He sighed. "You're good. You're kind. You have a good heart. You're not . . . . . . *this*. You're not someone who would hurt someone else. You're my *beautiful*, *sweet* Julie, who would put everyone else before herself. There isn't a part of you that would put harm on anyone. You're someone who loves with her whole being and someone who I'll always be in love with."

"Except, I'm *not*. I may have been her at one point, but that Julie is long gone, Dalton. It's like she never even existed." I began to pull him again as we began to walk further onto the trail. "That Julie faded away a long time ago. But you're right. She *was* good. She *was* kind. She *did* have a good heart. But that heart is filled with darkness now, and it's all because of you."

Chapter 18
Dalton 1997

The house was quiet without Roxy, Chad, and Sebastian fucking around, disturbing my sanctuary. I felt like I could relax, like I could breathe a little bit from all of the shit that was going on. With them being gone, it made me realize how suffocating they actually were. It was like I could never be alone in my own home because my so called "friends," these leeches, rarely left. And when they *were* gone, it wasn't very long before they would be back. I couldn't do the things I wanted to do, like write music or poetry. I couldn't be myself. They didn't know I had an interest in that kind of stuff. So it wasn't like I could just up and play the few notes I knew to inspire some lyrics. They would probably look at each other, then back at me like I was playing some joke on them. Then they would probably start to laugh at me in my own home. It wasn't like I could kick them out either, I know I had yelled at them to leave, but I knew they would eventually be back. Yeah they annoyed the shit out of me and didn't allow me to live to my full potential, but they were also the only real friends I had ever known. I wasn't the type to just turn my back on someone.

A few days of the unfamiliar silence passed when I heard a knock on my door. My heart fell to the pit of my stomach hoping it was who I wanted it to be, but of course it wasn't.

"What do you want?"

Sebastian nudged Chad in the arm. "Hey, I'm sorry about what happened with Julie. I was high and when Roxy told me what to do, I just did it. You know what she's like."

I stood there, listening to his pathetic apology, not wanting to talk, only wanting them to leave.

"Can we hang out here again, Dalton? We don't have anything else to do," Sebastian begged. "Julie's staying at Roxy's because her place got broken in to," he snickered. "And Roxy's in Palm Springs until tomorrow, so we don't want to go over there and . . . "

"You know what it's like over there," Chad said. "If her dad knew we were over, he'd kill us."

I continued to stand in front of these two men, listening to them plead to come back into my house, back into my life. It wasn't because they valued our friendship or wanted to hang out with me, it was because they had nothing better to do. That's the kind of guys Chad and Sebastian were. They would never make something of themselves. They would live off of their parents for the rest of their pathetic lives and their parents didn't care. Everything *my* father thought about *me* was actually true about *them*. They would never amount to anything. They would only live their lives on their father's payroll never knowing what it meant to have a dream or wanting a life other than what they had.

I looked them up and down, contemplating on whether or not I should let them in. I could have just slammed the door in their faces and turned them away, but knew there was a bigger picture here. I had to let them in so I could save the one person I loved. I stepped aside, gesturing for them to come in, but not without feeling pity for them. I was the best thing going on in their lives. That's pretty pathetic when you think of it.

Patting me on the shoulder, smiling from ear to ear, they headed to their designated spots on my couch. Sebastian grabbed the remote, Chad lit up a joint and they both laid back to an episode of Beavis and Butt-Head. The irony was too good.

I didn't say another word to them. I just walked out, heading to the only place I wanted to be . . . . . . with Julie.

My heart beat for her as she sat reading by the pool looking every bit of what I'd call perfection. I would have been a content man standing there watching her all day. She looked beautiful being alone in her own world. A world she was safe in. A world I wanted to be a part of instead of the one I was in now. I didn't want to disturb her, but I had to be near her. I also didn't mean to scare her, but holding her in my arms and feeling her heart race against my chest made me never want to leave her ever again. If fighting for her meant losing everything I had ever known, then that's what I needed to do.

As I held her in my arms, knowing what had happened to her, and how I couldn't fix it, all I could think of was how I *could* be there for her *now* as everything she ever needed. I would be there loving her in the only way I could, with *every-thing* I had.

We drove down to the beach, just the two of us, leaving behind the pressures from the city we lived in and the people we hung out with who judged us or had influence on the thing we were trying to build. It was the one time we were truly us.

We were real. We were who each of us needed, and we were falling in love.

I don't think two people were more perfect for each other than we were. You could feel how we were meant to be together in this complex moment in time where it felt like the entire world around us was a blur, and we were the only two people roaming around the earth. I kept thinking how could this be any more perfect? How could *she* be any more perfect? And then we were able to open up to each other in way that felt right.

"I never told anyone that before." She looked up at me and smiled. Looking into her eyes made me want everything she had talked about. The kids, a family, a home. It's funny how you could never know you want something until the right person comes along and says it. I wanted it all, and I wanted it all with her.

After hours spent on the beach, getting lost in each other's words, we headed back to the one place I didn't want Julie to step back into, Roxy's. I didn't want to leave her. I felt even more of a pull to protect her. The last thing I wanted was for Roxy to come back and somehow get into Julie's head and change how she felt about me. Letting her step out of my car and walk up to the front door was like mindlessly giving her back over to the lion's den. Who knew when we would see each other again? It could have been hours, it could have been days. It all depended on whether or not Roxy would allow it.

I know I keep repeating myself in how I should have fought harder for her. In this weird way of not doing anything, I thought I actually was. I should have done everything in my power to save her, to be with her, but I was too fucking stupid to open my mouth and take what I actually wanted. For whatever reason I couldn't get the words of how I felt about her, out of my mouth.

And as if she could read my mind, she stopped just as we got to the door. Before turning the handle and walking away from me, she looked back and asked me if I had to go. I couldn't stay fast enough.

Playing pretend in the life I wanted with Julie made me happy, like no matter what happened, everything would be complete because of her. Subconsciously I knew the situation I was in was serious, but for this fleeting moment, being with her, seeing her face, feeling her touch, hearing her beautiful laugh made me forget the real reason she had come into my life.

Time stood still then. I knew she could feel it too. It was like nothing had ever happened. We were just the two of us in a world where Roxy didn't even exist, we just so happened to be at her house. Spending time with Julie that night made the thought of what was possibly going to happen never even cross my mind. The stress suddenly seemed to have disappeared. I was able to just be a man spending time with the girl of my dreams.

"I'm hungry. Are you?" she asked.

"I could eat." The way she looked at me sent my heart into another dimension. She couldn't keep the smile off of my face even if she tried. "Wait." I pulled her into me and kissed her. The feeling of her being wrapped in my arms, my hands holding on to her body, not wanting to let it go made me almost have the courage to tell her how I felt. God, I can't believe how much I fucked up the best thing that's ever happened to me. She could be with me right now, in that little house she talked about, dancing in the kitchen, our kids crawling around. That could have been my fucking life, but instead . . . I'm here.

We went to the kitchen and I sat down watching her move so gracefully, with such ease, pulling things out of the refrigerator and placing them gently on the counter. The way she moved with intention to make me something, to take care of me, was something I never experienced before and I couldn't keep my eyes off of her.

"Okay, this is hands down the best sandwich I've ever had."

"Everything tastes better when someone else makes it for you." She smirked.

"That's true, but this one is way better than any other sandwich I've ever had made for me."

"Well," she lingered, "Okay, I may have a secret ingredient." She bit her lower lip as her cheeks began to flush. It took a lot of control to hold back my desire to grab her and bring her upstairs.

"And what's that?" I asked.

"If I tell you, then I'll have to kill you," she joked.

I tried to play it off like she was being cute, but it was a reminder of what was going to happen to Morgan, and whatever Roxy would end up doing to her. The remark was a blow bringing me back to reality from the rose-colored glasses I'd been wearing the entire evening. I had to save her. I had to stop Roxy.

I never let on that I actually knew what had happened to her a few nights before. I tried not to think about it either, because whenever I did, all I could think about was how I wanted to kill Chad.

I laid there though, as she drifted off to sleep in my arms, and I couldn't hold back what I wanted to tell her.

I apologized for not protecting her and when I tried to say the three words I'd never said to anyone before, the courage I thought I had earlier left, and they wouldn't come out. I don't know why they wouldn't. It's not like I didn't mean them. I also wasn't sure she would have even heard me. It was like if I said them, it would become real, and I didn't know what that would mean. I didn't know how I was going to be able to convince Roxy to not go through with it. I just didn't want to keep my feelings for her buried inside anymore. I wanted to wear her proudly on my arm and let the world know she was mine. Instead, I just watched her sleep peacefully in my arms, desperately feeling the words I couldn't say.

Chapter 19
Julie 2023

"Your screams still haunt me, you know." We only had to take a few more steps before reaching it, as a flashback played in my mind standing where I stood all those years before. "The funny thing is, is I knew I shouldn't have gone that night. Everything in me, except one little part, was telling me not to go."

"What was the little part?"

I laughed, reflecting on who I was back then. "That part was the stupid, immature, little girl, who just wanted to see you, even after you completely broke my heart."

He didn't say anything. He didn't have to. He knew he would always be in the wrong.

My bag dropped down onto the dirt next to me with a thud. "Now, let's see, where should we start?" I bent down, reaching in and pulling out a gun.

"Julie, what the fuck?" He scrambled backwards.

"I told you, I'm not the same person I used to be, Dalton." I looked at him, fully aware of what we were about to get into.

"Now, it's simple. You're going to have a choice." I

placed the gun down in front of him. "Well, it's not so much a choice as it is a decision."

"What are you talking about?"

"You were really convincing to me that night, Dalton. You really made me believe that you possibly cared about me. I mean, those *tears*. That *scream* for her to stop, but that was it. That was *all* you did when you could have done more."

His jaw clenched as he hung his head low.

"I know I keep repeating myself, but I'm trying to make a point. I want you to feel *everything* I had to endure and overcome because of you. Want to know why? Because I'll never be the same. Do you even comprehend that? Or is your self-righteous, 'I'm better than everybody' ego too thick for it to sink in? I can't move on with my life because *every day* I'm fighting to push past the mental torture I was in when I was in that interrogation room. Do you even get the magnitude of what that can do to someone? They *made me* believe I murdered Morgan. They repeatedly told me I was *lying* and that I needed to tell the truth and admit what I did. After a while of hearing them repeat the same things *over* and *over* again, I thought I was *actually* lying. I *fucking* believed it Dalton." My aggravation started to get the best of me. "Do you know the impact of what that can do to someone?" I started to laugh again. "Of course you don't because you're fucking *Dalton Blake* who everybody dotes on hand and foot. You always get the yes when you should be getting the fucking no. This is the perfect example right here, you're out of prison when you should be locked up forever rotting away with people just like you. So for you to *ever* think I'd be with you, just know this, *I've changed*. I'll *never* be who I once was. *Ever*."

Chapter 20
Dalton 1997

My mother never taught me how to care for someone else, how to do things for others, or help them out to make it easier. She only cared about herself and what people could do for *her*. Obviously, my father didn't teach me either, given we had a tumultuous relationship. I lived a life where everything was done for me. I was the poster boy for having it made. As dense as that sounds, I didn't think there was anything outside of living that way. To be honest, I didn't want to know another way either. That is until I met *her*.

Sure, it would have been easy for me to send my house-keepers to Julie's to fix the mess Chad and Sebastian made. God, those two were idiots. I don't know where they would be if they didn't have Roxy to order them around; probably higher than shit or being taken advantage of by people who didn't actually care about them.

I was still so pissed off at Chad for doing what he did to Julie. I don't know why I let him back into my life so quickly and so easily. I knew I felt bad for him, but maybe I also liked the comfort of his familiarity? Or maybe it's because deep down, I looked at him like a brother. So, for whatever fucking reason, I forgave him for doing the worst possible fucking thing to the girl I cared about more than anything. I don't know why I forgave him, it sounds pretty lame, but I'm not a shrink. I've never been to one. I probably should have, though.

Julie needed more from me than just taking her out those two times and not being by her side the entire night at The Viper Room. I needed to prove to her, and myself, that I was worthy of her love. So I decided I would do it myself. I wanted to show her I loved her without being able to say the words. I thought that doing something completely unexpected of me would show her that. It took a while because the two dipshits left it a wreck. They even shattered the picture frame with a photo of Julie and who I assumed was her grand-mother. You could see the love they had for one another on their faces and I couldn't help but remember what Julie had said at the beach, how her grandmother would have loved me. I placed the glassless frame on the table and moved on to clean up around her phone.

There were crumpled up papers littering the floor and countertop, but I stopped when something caught my eye. As I knelt down to get a better look, I couldn't help but smile. There were a few pieces of paper with doodles all over them and in Julie's perfect handwriting, 'Mrs. Dalton Blake,' 'Julie Blake,' 'Dalton + Julie,' covered the pages. Seeing it made my heart start to pound in my chest, the smile on my face growing wider, feeling like I was on top of the world with the girl in my life who I knew was going to be the one to take my name. I couldn't help it, and pocketed a few of them because these weren't just doodles, they were practice for what was to come.

Reality hit later that night when I was at home, relaxing from working hard on the cleanup. Chad and Sebastian were faded, watching TV on my couch, when all of a sudden, a familiar laugh echoed throughout the halls. Anger instantly rose up inside me. Sure enough, as I walked into my living room, there she was, sitting in-between the guys, snorting a line.

"Get out, Roxy."

"Are you sure you really want to do that, Dalton?" she expressed through narrowed eyes. "I'm not so sure that's a good idea, seeing as how I know *everything* about you." She cocked her head with a devilish grin on her face.

Chad looked to Sebastian. "What the fuck?" he mouthed.

Sebastian shrugged. He was none the wiser.

She had me, again, in a position where I didn't know which way to go or which person to save. There was the way I knew I should have gone, but I was torn in the hold she had over me. For what? I don't know why it mattered to me as much as it did. If she destroyed me, I would get over it. I could move on with my life without my name protecting me. What *did* matter was her destroying Julie and I was too . . . cowardly to do anything about it. The thing that bothered me the most was I couldn't understand why.

My dad had been nothing but a dick to me my entire life, never thinking I was good enough. Yet still, for some fucked up reason I had to make sure he would be okay. It wasn't like I was afraid of him or anything, I just didn't want to be the one responsible for ruining his life. I knew he would probably never find out who did it, but he would definitely find a way to blame me. That's what he'd always done. He blamed his downfall on me. He said losing his vision was because I caused him so many problems that he had to always fucking worry about me messing up and causing problems for his family. Not *our* family, *his*.

"You're never going to do anything with your life. You're

a waste of a son," he'd say to me. Then at parties, or events, wherever he needed to show face and be seen, it was always, "Oh, Dalton, he's got everything going for him. You've seen him around, always a beautiful girl on his arm. You know who he gets that from, right?" He'd laugh, boastfully, as if I were this perfect son he could be proud of. He never was though, and he never would be.

I walked out of the room outraged I had let Roxy and her delusional perception of herself control me like that. Everything in me wanted to yell at her, to scream for her not to do this. I wanted to fucking tell her I loved Julie, but knew if I did, it would somehow make her go over the edge and destroy everything in front of her.

I should have known better. I should have reminded myself that Roxy wasn't stupid. She knew I was in love with Julie. She knew it. You can always tell when someone you've known your entire life falls in love. They act different. They look different. Although I felt like the façade of being who I usually was in front of her was convincing enough, she could still tell. That's what friends do. They know everything about you.

"Hey, Dalton!" She walked in like nothing ever happened, a different disposition than she had displayed earlier in my living room. I couldn't stand being anywhere near her so I had been hiding out in my bedroom writing some poetry, maybe a song, about how Julie made me feel, trying to distract myself from the turmoil Roxy had created inside of me. So, you could imagine how angry I got when my beautiful distraction was interrupted by the unwanted company of a soon to be fallen friend.

"What do you want, Roxy?"

"Aww, what's with the pouty face, Dalton? You know I don't like to be around pathetic things." She walked in and got on the bed, nuzzling up next to me. "I know what you need." She started to run her hand along my chest making her way towards the button of my jeans.

"Stop." I pushed her hand away.

"Come on, Dalton. Don't you want to play with me?" Her voice was now childlike. "It'll be fun! It always is. Besides, I know you need it. I haven't seen you with anyone for a few weeks now. All of that pent up aggression must be *aching* at you for release." She caressed her hand over my jeans again, biting her lower lip in a crazed manner.

"I said to stop, Roxy. Go bother Chad or Sebastian." I shrugged her off harder.

"I can't."

"Why?"

"Because I want *you*," she cooed. "And besides," she pouted her lower lip, "They left."

"Why didn't you go with them?"

Her pout turned into a smile filled with mischief along with a gaze full of fire. "Because I live here, duh!"

"I let you *stay* here. That doesn't mean you *live* here."

"Okay, Dalton. Whatever you say." She smirked.

"What's with you?"

"Nothing. I just—" She started to kiss the nape of my neck. "I just want you." She looked into my eyes seductively, like she wanted to get the sexual fix she needed to feel good about herself again.

"Roxy," I groaned, slightly. "Stop." I pushed her away, again.

"Playing hard to get only makes me want you more." Her slow tone hit the right nerve as she sat on top of me, pushing me down when I tried to get up. "Come on, please?!"

She was acting like a child, trying to get her way. It was as if she didn't have me right then, her whole world would start to cave in. But I didn't want her, even though something was telling me I did.

She bent over, her mouth near my ear. "I think you want me too. In fact, I *know* you do," she whispered as she reached down touching my hardened cock.

"Roxy," I groaned.

"What, Dalton?" Her voice was soft and breathy. "Do you still want me to stop?"

I should have had her stop. I should have listened to my heart, but my dick was telling me otherwise.

She was making it impossible. The urge to have completely meaningless sex came over me and I shot up, turning her over and throwing her down, the both of us ripping the clothes off of one another, trying to get a quick release.

I'm not proud of giving in to her the way I did. I'm not proud that this was the only way I felt like I had dominance over her. But there was nothing that would have ever prepared me for what happened next. It was almost as if it were planned because the timing was right too perfect.

"Julie!" I had to run through the shattered glass from the bottle of champagne smashed on the floor, trying to hold up the sheet I had around me. "Julie! Julie!"

I heard a thud and tried to run faster, but the pain from a piece of glass pierced my foot, making me fumble. I couldn't catch her. She was already out of the driveway by the time I got to the door.

"FUCK!"

I sat in the kitchen for a minute to try and alleviate the throbbing in my foot. "Fuck!" My face fell in my hands. Roxy was devious, but I didn't realize just how far she would go to get what she wanted. She wanted Julie to hate me, to make it easier for me to keep in line with her plan and let the one thing I wanted more than anything in this world slip away from me without any hesitation. But I couldn't let that happen. I wasn't *going* to let it happen.

I confronted her when I got back to my room, bursting through the door like a man on a mission to save the woman I loved.

"Leave Julie the fuck alone, Roxy."

"And why would I do that?" She narrowed her eyes on me.

"You fucking know why."

She stared at me, waiting for me to falter, but I stood my ground to protect the woman I loved.

"Ugh, fine. I'll figure something else out."

I took her statement as her figuring something else out to do to Morgan. That she was done with everything. That she wouldn't need Julie anymore, but I was wrong. I was fucking *dead* wrong.

Chapter 21
Julie 2023

Abreeze picked up, filling the air around us with an exhilarating feeling of anxiousness. The hair on the back of my neck began to rise as goosebumps formed on my arms. It was a sign, like the universe was agreeing with what I was doing. It was giving me approval. Letting me know I was doing the right thing. I could feel it and knew he felt it too.

"We're going to play a little game now, Dalton. I've already told you there would be a choice, but should we make it a little more fun?"

He was fidgeting with the ties around his wrists, uncomfortable, wanting to be anywhere but there, I'm sure. That's exactly how I wanted it. "Now, the game is simple. I'm going to ask you a question and you're going to answer honestly. Can you do that?"

He cleared his throat, "Yes."

"Good. Now if I feel like you're not telling me the truth . . . . . . then you'll have to make your choice. So, really it's all up to you Dalton on whether or not you live or die."

The energy between us shifted. His body began to stiffen,

unsure of what his outcome would be. So much of who I was had changed since he and I first met and now he had no idea what kind of person I'd become.

As the intensity in my eyes glistened, a smile formed across my face. Not knowing what the outcome would be gave me a form of satisfaction in knowing *I* had all of the control.

I was no longer the Julie he thought he was in love with. I was now the Julie he created into being his worst nightmare.

Chapter 22
Dalton 1997

She wouldn't answer when I tried calling, and I was too afraid to leave a message. There were even some nights I would park outside of her apartment, just sitting there looking up at her window, waiting, watching; hoping to catch a glimpse of her walking past.

I had messed up again. I knew that. I thought that by giving her space, it would somehow help erase everything she saw even though I knew it wouldn't be easy for her to forget. One day I even went by her job at Musso and Franks to catch the slightest glimpses of her through the door. There was this aura she gave off, this feeling of me needing her to be in my life. Since my car wasn't exactly incognito, I borrowed Chad's a couple of times to follow her home to make sure she got there safely. Waiting for her to come back to me was the hardest thing I had ever done in my life. You would think trying to stop Roxy would be—and it was— but this was harder. I should have just let her go, but feeling like I lost her was like getting my heart torn from my chest. The thing is, to stop Roxy I just needed the balls to stand up to her. But with Julie, and feeling like I lost her, I had to figure out how to get her back. This was a place I had never been before. I couldn't lose her. She was mine.

I could have done the cliché thing and send her flowers with an apology note, but figured she'd throw them away as soon as they were delivered. Aimlessly standing outside of her window with a boom box over my head, playing the song from our first date, would probably lead her to calling the cops telling them there was a lunatic harassing her. I even considered sending Chad and Sebastian over to her apartment to check on her, but I didn't want Julie to go into a state of shock in case she suddenly remembered it was Chad who had done that horrible thing to her. I kept trying to think of what to do, of what I could say. Then one night, she showed up. I thought I heard her name being said from the living room, and when I went to check, I was right. She was there.

I was like a teenager again. My hormones were raging, excited my crush was in the same vicinity as me. I was a lucky son of a bitch that the woman I was in love with reappeared back into my life and I just couldn't contain my feelings any longer. I walked right up to her, a smile beaming on my face, trying to give her a kiss, but she turned away from me, leaving me heartbroken and distraught. There I was standing like a dumb idiot not thinking she was even mad at me, but of course she was. It took me a second to realize she wasn't there for me; she was there for Roxy.

I left the room heading towards the kitchen, giving her more of the space I was already trying to give her. I had to get her alone somehow. She needed to hear me out and listen to what I had to say because my side of the story could change her mind. She needed to know that I only wanted *her*, not Roxy.

Her not-so-subtle hint of not wanting to be near me was heard. But that didn't stop me from still trying to get her attention. I figured I'd set something up out by the pool in the hopes of recreating the night we spent together on the beach. Getting her to remember who I really was and how we felt when we were together would make her want to talk to me. It had to. I had champagne chilling in an ice bucket along with some candles burning to lighten the mood. The setup looked nice and inviting. It was the perfect gesture to turn what was an already fucked situation into one where she could hopefully forgive me.

As soon as I walked back inside, something didn't feel right. I made my way to the living room and was instantly hit with an uneasiness seeing her chair empty, thinking I had lost her again, but this time for good. The feeling only grew worse when I realized Chad and Sebastian weren't sitting on the couch either. Something was going on. And of course, all I could think of was what Chad had done to her before. Where had they gone? Where had they taken her?

I was frantic, looking around downstairs, calling her name, "Julie?" They weren't answering. I headed to the front door, praying they hadn't just up and left. Thankfully, Chad's car was still out front and I was able to let out a sigh of relief.

Still not knowing where they were, there was only one place left to check. I made my way to the end of the hallway and that's when I heard a commotion coming from upstairs. My heart sank to the pit of my stomach. Without hesitation I ran taking the stairs in two's to get to her faster. Whatever was going on, I knew wasn't going to be good for her, for me, for any of us.

We collided and I caught her in my arms as she was rushing past me, tears streaming down her cheeks. Her face was flushed and she appeared scared, like someone was about to hurt her. She started screaming at me how I was the worst one, that I didn't help her. *What the fuck had Roxy told her?* I tried to console her the best I could, hugging her, comforting her, hoping she would calm down. The woman I loved was in distress and no matter how many times I tried telling her everything would be okay, she wouldn't listen.

Roxy had finally done it. She had taken this further than it needed to go. It was already visibly clear Julie would never be the same. My sweet, beautiful Julie would never be who I fell in love with. She had lost her innocence in the short time she had been in our lives and it was all because of that fucking bitch. So, I did the one thing I didn't want to do. The one thing I was trying to not let happen. I let her go . . . hoping she'd be gone forever. I knew that as much as I loved her, if I never saw her again, I would know she was safe and alive. It wasn't her fault she naïvely got mixed up in our fucked up world of having too much freedom and no one there to tell us no. She was too good of a person to be there. She deserved everything good life had to offer, and I wouldn't have been able to give it to her.

Roxy came storming into the hall. Her shoulders pulled back, her chin lifted in confidence, her eyes completely dark, feeding off the attack she had just placed on Julie. The adrenaline giving her the last bit of confidence to carry out her plan. "It's happening. Tonight," she affirmed.

"What? No! You can't do this, Roxy."

"Are you trying to stop me, Dalton?" She cocked her head, her eyes narrowing before returning to a smile. "Yeah that's right. You don't have it in you. I'm calling Morgan to come over and I'm telling Chad and Sebastian to leave. Tonight's the night!" Her brow raised as a seductive look of evil formed on her face. I'm not one to frighten easy, but that look was the most fucking terrifying thing I had ever seen. That look said it all. She meant business, and the only thing I could do was hope Julie wouldn't answer when she would inevitably make the call that would change all of our lives, forever.

An hour later, Morgan was at my house.

"What do you want, Roxy? You haven't talked to me in months and now, all of a sudden, you call me out of the blue to hang out? It doesn't make any sense. I didn't think we were friends after I turned you in, and honestly, I don't even know why I'm here."

Roxy put on her "friend" act. The one she'd always done with Morgan and most recently with Julie. "I just wanted to thank you, Morgan."

"For what?" She was firm in her questioning, knowing she most likely wouldn't be able to believe what Roxy was about to say.

"For what?!" She laughed. "For saving my life, Morg! You really helped me. I'm happy, I'm full of life and I'm *clean* because of you." The false sincerity in her voice made her appear even crazier than I already thought she was. I couldn't tell if she was just high or if she had actually lost her mind. Roxy needed help and all of us were too shitfaced, by drugs or the fear of her wrath, to see it.

"That's not what I heard."

"And what was that exactly?"

"That you haven't changed. You're still using."

"That's so funny! You're so funny, Morgan!"

"I can tell you're high right now, I'm not stupid, Roxy. You're not a nice person when you're high."

"Then why did you come over when I called if I'm not a nice person?"

"Because I wanted to give you the benefit of the doubt. I

had to see it for myself. Obviously, I was hoping you were clean, even though I knew you weren't. I still care about you as a person, Roxy, I'm not that heartless. There's still a part of me that cares for you as a friend as stupid as that sounds. I have plans for my life and it's not to sit back and live off of my father, getting high just to feel something, or nothing. So there's no need to hang out with you guys. No offense, Dalton," she assured me before turning back to Roxy. "I should be studying instead of wasting my time doing God knows what else."

In a perfect world, Morgan would have said she didn't want to be friends anymore. She would have walked right out the front door, leaving us behind. Most importantly, she would continue to live. But as much as every part of my being was hoping that would have happened, it didn't.

It wasn't fair. Morgan had a future planned for herself. Everyone knew she wasn't like us. She had something more in her than just a trust fund. She had determination and drive to find purpose and meaning for her life. She was good, just like my Julie.

Instead of telling her to leave, or warning her in some way, I just stood there, not moving as some pseudo way to protect her. Again, Roxy's hold on me was causing me to become someone I didn't think I was. As for Morgan, who was much stronger of a person than me, it would have been so easy. She could have just walked the fuck out of our lives. Why couldn't she have just done that?

"Okay, well since you're here, what would you say about going to our favorite spot one last time? You know, for old times' sake?"

"Roxy, come on," I sighed, when I was finally able to speak, but the words I should have said were still trapped in my mind unable to form in my mouth.

"Dalton, she's already here." She smiled at Morgan. "Come on, what do you say? Just one last time, and then after that we'll never have to see each other again."

I looked to Morgan, trying to plead with her with my expression to say no. I knew what Roxy was actually saying, but that stupid fucking lump in my throat refrained me from telling her to run. Thoughts were rapid firing in my brain. If I had to stop this, which I did need to do, this would be the time. Something inside of me was finally willing to stand up for myself, for them.

"Roxy, stop. We're not doing th— . . . "

Her look cut through my words like the razor sharp knife she had repeatedly stabbed me in my back with since she came up with this fucking idea.

"Fine. Whatever. Let's go," Morgan said. "One last time, and then I never want to see you again, Roxy. And it won't be hard either. I'm moving to New York soon."

Roxy's expression turned devious. "Perfect!"

We walked outside, my keys rattling in my hand from the nerves. The three of us got into my car and as I started the engine, it backfired. A loud POP, sounding like a gunshot, had Morgan screaming and myself jumping in my seat, but Roxy remained calm. If I didn't know any better, I'd say it even egged her on for what was about to happen.

The drive was silent, and tension filled the small space. Morgan didn't want to be there. I didn't either. I kept telling myself I wouldn't let it happen. I was going to stop her. She hadn't exactly told me her plan, so all I could do was assume she was going to push her over the side somewhere and let a hiker find the body. That would be easy. It was clean and could happen to anybody who wasn't paying attention. All I would have to figure out was how to not have the blame placed on Julie. I didn't know why I had been so worried before, the perfect solution was laid out before me. I would have to push Roxy over the side of the trail before she could get to Morgan. I would take the fall, and both Morgan and Julie would be free to live their lives. It was the perfect plan, except I was wrong. Underestimating Roxy was the biggest mistake I could have ever made.

"What a beautiful night!" Roxy exclaimed, pulling my attention from surveying the path to see where I could push her over and looking out onto the view of our city. The night was beautiful, but only in the way beauty can be eerie. Everything seemed to be still, and the air was calm, not a cloud in the sky, the feeling of knowing something bad is about to happen looming over us, or maybe just me.

I was nervous. I'd never wanted to kill anyone before. Yeah, I made remarks about it, but people do that sometimes when they're angry. I never actually wanted to do it or wanted to know what it felt like. To be responsible for ending someone's life and having to live with that for the rest of yours? Who would want to do that? A fucking crazy person who needed some serious psychological help that's who. Fucking Roxy.

As the three of us stood there, looking out, I caught Roxy's expression from the corner of my eye. She was that thirteen-year-old girl again, looking as if she were on top of the world ready to take it head on. But all hope was lost when Morgan spoke and the quick glimpse of who Roxy once was faded. My heart sunk because reality hit and I knew I'd never see her again.

"Okay, we're here. This is great," Morgan said, sarcastically. "Now, let's go."

"Why do you want to leave so soon, Morgan? We just got here. Besides this is the end of an era, saying goodbye to each other for good. Let's savor it a little."

"Roxy, I don't want to be here as much as you don't want to be here, let's just leave." She let out a huff. "This is ridiculous. We're adults, we're not children anymore. We can be civil with each other, that's fine, but we both know we aren't friends anymore. I don't think we ever really were."

This was it. This was my shot. My one and only chance to make this all right. Morgan was a few feet ahead of Roxy with Roxy's back being turned away from me. Everything was set up as if it was meant to be. I started to charge towards her, my arms outstretched in front of me when I was suddenly stopped dead in my tracks with a dizzying ringing in my ears. My hands went straight to cover them and I lost control of my footing, causing me to stumble backwards, barely able to catch myself. When I was finally able to open my eyes, I saw Roxy holding a gun mere inches away from me.

"Holy shit! I did it!" Her eyes lit up. "I fucking did it!" Her voice, muffled through the buzzing.

It took a few seconds for me to get stable on my feet, and as I did, the initial shock of what had just happened hit me. "What the fuck, Roxy?"

"I did it! *We* did it!" She stood there, almost like she was admiring what she'd done, giving herself praise for such a heinous act.

"Morgan." I ran to her, breaking down when I saw the puddle of blood surrounding her. I could hear Roxy mumbling something in the background, but my focus was on my lifeless friend and the beautiful life she had, just moments before. The realness of it all, and how I could have prevented this ending, started to pour out of me. I had been holding on to so much stress because of what Roxy had over me and not wanting to turn her in for the fear of losing everything I had. I couldn't help but release what I had been holding in.

My sobs were interrupted as she shoved her portable phone in my face, bringing me back to a harsh reality that her plan wasn't fully over. There was still the part I dreaded most. Framing the love of my life, Julie. "Here. Call her."

Something in me finally ignited what I had been trying to do for the past couple of months. "No, Roxy. I won't let you do this to her, to Julie. Look what you just did to Morgan," I cried. "You've lost it. You've completely lost it."

"DO IT! And get her to come or *you'll* be next," she said, pointing the gun against my head.

As fast as that courage came, it was gone. I trembled, trying to punch in Julie's phone number, not being able to see the numbers from the tears welling up in my eyes. The feeling of being helpless in what could have otherwise been a heroic situation where I saved the day, saving the innocent bystander from the evil villain in a Shakespearian tragedy, washed over me. But I wasn't that. I wasn't a hero. I was weak and afraid to go against the one person in my life I thought I was closest to for the fear of having my father's name tarnished and my life ruined even though that's what I said I had wanted. I *would* rather have my life ruined instead of Julie's. It's just . . . not what happened. I wasn't able to be the man I always thought myself to be which is why I'll always blame myself for the rest of my life. My father was right about me. I would never amount to anything. I was worthless.

Her beautiful voice echoed through the phone, and I

choked on my words. How could I be responsible for such an awful thing to happen to two beautiful, smart women? These women had *everything* going for them, except for the fact that each one of them knew and befriended a psychotic killer.

When I wouldn't speak, Roxy cocked the gun against my forehead, forcing the word I didn't want to say to come out, "Julie."

Chapter 23
Julie 2023

"Okay, first question, Dalton. This one isn't going to be too much of a doozy." I paused, looking down at him, noticing my shadow the moon had casted on the ground behind him. I looked like a monster out to get my prey, but I knew I didn't look like one. I looked like the girl of his dreams except I was the one in his worst nightmare. "Why did you go along with Roxy's plan?"

He took a deep breath in, letting it out slowly. "You didn't know her, or the *real* her, just what she wanted you to see. Growing up, she commanded everyone's attention in any way she could. We all put that attention on her because she was the only girl in our little group. We kind of let her have the leadership role over us. I know that sounds dumb. We kind of hated her, but loved her at the same time." He cleared his throat. "Our lives weren't what they looked like from the outside. We were real people dealing with a lot of the same shit everybody else does. Like our fucked up relationships with our parents, not being taken seriously because of who we are or where we came from. We just had money thrown at us to cover up whatever messed up shit we got into. When you come from the kind of life we did, where you're not really loved or cared about by anyone, you make your own family. That's what Roxy, Chad, and Sebastian were to me at one point. We were a family. Until we weren't."

He looked up at me. His rugged good looks which I had once fallen head over heels for, were now being shown to me under the moonlight, sending my heart back to a place I didn't want it to be.

"I never told you what Roxy had over me. I don't know why I even cared so much about it. It's not like my dad ever cared about me, but I felt a need to protect him. Which is some bullshit I made up in my mind because the only person who actually, *truly,* cared about me was the *one* person who loved me. The one person who I should have protected the entire time. I was too stupid in thinking if I did this for my family, for my father, he would somehow realize I was worthy of his love." He started to laugh at himself. "I regret every day agreeing to go along with Roxy and her plan for the fear of her exposing this mythical hero I thought my father to be. I went along with it all before I met you."

"So if it was someone else, would you have gone through with it guilt free?" After saying all of those things, revealing his truth, I was curious to know if he would have done the same thing under different circumstances, which was absolutely nothing.

"I don't know."

I took a deep inhale.

"I'm just being honest, Julie. I know what she wanted to do was wrong, but I was too afraid to be the one to lose everything for my family. You don't know what my dad is like. What he expected of me and never got. He's a fucking bastard, but still was someone who I wanted to be proud of me. So, I agreed to go along with what she was going to do, never really thinking she would actually go through with it. I also never expected it to be *you.* You kind of just appeared at the wrong time, and I never thought I would actually fall in love with you. But that was before I saw your beautiful face that day at the diner. When I looked at you it was like my whole world finally made sense and I knew I had to have you and that I had to try and stop her. I just . . . ”

“You just what?”

He was quiet for a second. “I didn't try hard enough.”

We were both silent, taking in the words from the sob story he was telling to try and sway me into understanding his viewpoint. No matter how he explained it, there was still no explanation, believable enough, as to why he didn't do anything for me, someone he claimed to have changed his life. Someone he claimed to be in love with . . . . . . but he never continued.

“Okay, question number two. Were you in love with her?”

“What the?! NO. Why would you even think that?”

“Umm, I don't know, Dalton, maybe because I caught you sleeping with her.”

“You've got to be kidding me. She manipulated me too, Julie.” His face was somber. I didn't know if I could believe him or not. He sighed heavily. “Throughout the years, we'd sleep together every once in a while, but it was just sex to get that release, to feel good, you know?”

“I *don't* know actually. I was a virgin, and I was I was saving myself for someone special because that's what I thought people did. I was waiting for someone I was in love with, and I thought that someone was going to be *you.* I was *prepared* for it to be you. But I had that taken away from me when she had me raped by Chad. Since then, I haven't been able to let a man get near me, let alone touch me. So no, I don't know that release, Dalton.”

He shifted his position, feeling uncomfortable with my words. "The day I met you, I knew you were the only woman I wanted to be with, and I stopped being with other women. But that night when you walked in on us, she had come on to me and that urge took over. I tried to refuse. I even pushed her off of me a few times, but she kept coming on to me, forcing me to do it."

I scoffed.

"I know that's not an excuse, but as a man, when that urge starts to rise, it's almost impossible to stop. I know I should have stopped. Especially because I really didn't want to do it. I kept telling her no, but she kept forcing it on me."

"Wait." I held my hand up to stop him. "Are you trying to compare yourself to me?"

"No, I . . . "

"Because it kind of sounds like you are."

I could see the frustration building in him. "No, I let it happen. I gave in to my resistance and I willingly had sex with her. I did it because I was afraid that if I didn't, she would expose what she had against me. I was scared, Julie. Is that what you want me to say? That I'm a coward? Because I'll yell it for everyone to hear. I'M A FUCKING COWARD. DALTON BLAKE IS A FUCKING COWARD."

A smile crossed my face. "I guess you just answered my third question."

His jaw was quivering as tears filled his eyes, doing what men typically did when trying not to show emotion for the fear of being vulnerable. But then one released and rolled down his cheek. "And what question was that?"

"Why didn't you protect me?"

He huffed out a laugh. His eyes filled with more water, still trying to hold back his cry. Through his sniffs, he managed to say, "I should have done everything I could have to protect you, Julie. God, I fucked up. That's the only regret I have in life, and I wish I could go back and change it. I wish I could make things different. Make *me* different, but I can't. So I'm left being this worthless piece of shit that couldn't save the woman I love. I don't know . . . " He tilted his head towards the ground and released what he'd been holding in. "I just know it wasn't supposed to be like that."

Chapter 24
Dalton 1997

I told her the truth about how being with Roxy was a mistake, but she didn't want to hear any of it. Her voice through the muffled receiver was upset, which was honorable because who wouldn't be mad after what she had already gone through at the hands of Roxy. If she could have only seen me though, knelt down with a gun to my head, terrified that if I didn't get her to come I would end up just like Morgan, lying on the ground in front of me. As much as I didn't want to be on the phone with her, the sound of her voice made me feel calm even though I was having an internal battle with what I had just witnessed and what I was being forced to do. I'm guilty for using the way she felt about me to my advantage and it makes me sick to think about every fucking day. I could have yelled, 'Run away Julie. Run far away from here and never think twice about it. Go live your life, your beautiful life and think of me often. I love you. God, I fucking *love* you with my *entire* being. If I could just hold you forever in my arms, I would. I would love you and cherish you, and worship the ground you walked on until my very last day. Run Julie, run away from here and never look back.' Instead, I told her the one thing that would make her at least question coming. I told her that she was my girl, *my girl*, because she *was* and always would be. Thankfully she didn't listen, and I was left somewhat at ease when she hung up the phone. But all I was left with was hoping she wouldn't come. I was left hoping that was the last time I would ever hear from her.

I began praying to God, something I never did before, that she wouldn't show up. I prayed that somehow, she had finally come to her senses. That she finally realized just how evil Roxy really was. After I prayed, all I could do was wait, hoping my prayers came true and she wouldn't show up. Then my own thoughts became riddled with the uncertainty of what Roxy would actually do to me if Julie did show up, or worse, if she didn't.

"Everything's working out just how I planned it," she said, snorting her motivation. "God that was such a rush. You should try it, Dalton. I've never felt so alive."

She may have felt alive, but I felt sick. Hearing her speak of how she had just taken the life of not only someone who was underserving of it, but someone who was nice and kind, made me want to vomit. Morgan had meaning to her life. She had purpose. She was someone who cared for the well-being of others, her friends. Roxy destroyed all of that because she was so unhappy with herself that she had to take it out in the most violent way on the only person who ever actively tried to get her help.

She had finally gone too far. It wasn't all fun and games like I thought she had made it seem. I guess I just never actually believed she would do it . . . and then she did.

All of a sudden, I started to panic. The shock of what was happening hit me all at once that Morgan was dead, Roxy killed her and Julie could very well be next. I was beside myself. I couldn't really think straight and started pacing back and forth muttering out ideas of how to get Julie out of this. My dad didn't matter anymore, I had finally come to a point where I was ready to have whatever was going to come . . . come. My only focal point was figuring out how to get Julie out of this. But everything was happening in this weird motion of slowness, yet rapidly happening at the same time. My sense of time was shifted while being trapped in my mind of trying to come up with a way to have this all fall on the person who actually did it, to Roxy. I was too into my own thoughts that I didn't even realize she *had* shown up.

When I saw her walking towards me, I was stunned she was actually there. Then again it didn't surprise me because she was a good person. She would be there for a friend even if that friend stabbed her in the back time and time again. That's just who she was. She was good.

Then I met her eyes, her beautiful eyes, and saw the face that made me fall in love with her. It felt like a dream. I couldn't decipher if this was reality or not. I just remember seeing her and thinking, 'She shouldn't have come.'

Chapter 25
Julie 2023

S eeing him in such a vulnerable state, weak and remorseful, triggered something in me. Maybe I felt bad for him, or maybe it could have been pity, but it was a feeling I knew all too well. Only this time, I was on the other side of it. In the contemplating thoughts I had I could see the old Julie matching his feelings and apologizing for what she was putting him through. Her feelings were from the love she still had for him whereas the new Julie, the one I let take over, only saw how weak of a man he really was and used that to fuel my plot of revenge.

"You know, I thought you were going to be the man I was going to spend the rest of my life with. I thought you were this cocky, holier-than-thou guy who knew he could get anybody, and for some reason, that only made me want you more. Yet, somehow, I thought *I* was the lucky one you chose to grace your presence with. You *chose* to have me be the girl in your life. The girl who you would let love you. The girl you could be yourself with, not the façade you put on for everyone of being the dark, mysterious, bad boy every girl wanted. You could be the smart, sensitive, creative and loving guy you truly were. Now, both of those sides of you which once had me willing and *wanting* to give you everything, every part of me, is completely turned off by how much of a pathetic loser you actually are. I mean, you said it yourself, you're a coward." I crouched down to meet his gaze, knowing by the look on his face that he wanted to say something, but knew nothing he could say would matter. He already admitted his faults. So what empty words would have made a difference? "Now this round is going to be all the more fun." I winked.

He didn't flinch, but being as close to him as I was, I saw a few more tears fall from his eyes. "Julie."

"You're really not a very good listener, are you?"

"Come on. Just stop this."

"Wow! See how easy those words can come out? 'Just stop this.' If only you would have said them then." I cocked my head into a smirk.

"I did."

"Sure," I laughed.

"I did say something like that to her. I told her to leave you alone. I told her you were a nice girl, and she shouldn't go through with it."

"How do I know you're telling me the truth?"

"I would never lie to you, Ju . . . " he caught himself on the start of my name.

I started to laugh again. "But you did, Dalton. You did lie to me."

"Not telling you something and lying are two different things."

"Is that what you tell yourself so you can sleep at night?" I waited for him to answer. "Oh, God! The incomparable Dalton Blake, everyone! Acting like he knows the difference between lying and telling the truth." I smirked. "Not saying anything is a lie of omission. They may be different, but they accomplish the same thing. Hiding the truth."

"Julie," trepidation coated his voice.

"Okay, it's time to make your choice. You've humored me enough."

He looked at me, silence filling his face once again.

"It's really simple, Dalton. Your choice. You have to choose if you're going to be the one to kill yourself or if you're going to take the cowards' way out, *again*, and make me do it."

Chapter 26
Dalton 1997

The way my breath caught in my throat when I realized what Roxy was about to do next is a feeling I know I'll never forget. My life, or the life I was hoping to have flashed before my eyes before I could even comprehend what was happening. The experiences of a life not yet lived, were taken away from me seeing Roxy aim the gun at the back of Julie's head, slowing inching her way with a sadistic smile on her face, prepared to pull the trigger. Her words of wanting to feel what it felt like again bounced around my head, only this time it would be my Julie.

"NO!"

I really thought my yell would have stopped her. Like she'd hear it in my voice, my pain, my fear, my love for Julie, but the crazed look in her eyes was unlike anything I'd ever seen. Her eyes were dark and reminiscent of someone who had tasted death and needed to have another bite. This wasn't the girl I knew my entire life. Looking at her now was like looking at a completely different person.

Roxy kept walking towards Julie who still had no idea she was being ambushed by someone she thought was her friend.

The gun was held steady, outstretched in Roxy's hands, with her finger on the trigger. It was all happening in slow motion as I braced myself for what I was about to witness. As much as I tried to force myself to move and push Julie out of the way taking the bullet to my own chest, I was stuck, frozen, in fear or shock.

And then, all of a sudden, Julie went down.

I'm not sure what made Roxy think twice about not pulling the trigger, I'm just grateful she didn't. I glanced up and saw the handle of the gun covered in blood and after that everything kind of became a blur.

I remember falling to Julie's side, cradling her unmoving body, trying to stop the blood from coming out of her head.

I thought I lost her.

The love of my life was now lying lifeless in my arms and all I could do was cry my heart out, finally able to express to her how I felt even though it was too late. "I love you, Julie. I love you. I'm so sorry, Julie. I'm so sorry. I love you." I kept repeating the words that had always been too hard to say, hoping somehow she'd hear me.

I never wanted it to get that far. I never meant for it too, at least, and I'll hate myself for the rest of my life knowing I didn't do more to try and stop it from happening.

"Get in the car, Dalton," Roxy yelled, but I couldn't move from Julie's side. How could I? She was all I'd ever wanted, and she was taken away from me because I didn't deserve her. "Get in the fucking car, Dalton. NOW!"

It was like I was in a trance, my mind blank, unable to think. I could barely breathe. I thought Roxy had killed Julie too. I was taking in her face, the way her lips were parted, remembering how they felt against mine. I didn't want to leave her. I didn't think I could.

Now that Roxy had finally done what she wanted to do,

it's like I woke up and realized I didn't want anything to do with her anymore. She had become a different person to me and I should have realized it sooner and left years before. She became someone I couldn't even look in the eye. Her soul was gone, and I wished she would have just killed herself back then before involving me in this mess. But then again, if she did do that, I would have never met, and lost, Julie. Having Julie in my life, even though it was for such a short period of time and for terrible reasons, made me realize the impact she had on me, and how every second of the time we spent together was worth it. *Not* having her in my life, didn't make sense to me. I didn't know how I would ever go on. How could I go on without the one who actually made my heart beat?

"Julie, I'm so sorry. I'm going to fix this. I promise. Please forgive me. Please! I'm going to make this right. I love you, Julie. I'm in love with you. Please forgive me."

The drive back to my house was filled with the loudest silence. I didn't even need to say what I wanted, she knew and left right away. My heart was completely shattered, and I became completely checked out from the world. All I could do was continuously picture Julie's lifeless body and how I had just left it behind. Even after everything happened, I was such a coward in not doing anything about it. I could have still done something to avenge her death, to have Roxy own up to what she had done. But I didn't do anything. Not a goddamn *fucking* thing.

I knew murdering Morgan, or being a part of it, would change me, and it did. I never wanted to murder anyone. The thought never crossed my mind, *ever*, until that day when

Roxy asked me about it. Even then, I lied. I never wanted to know what it would feel like. Who wants that, or even thinks that way? But now that I was a part of it, it was not a feeling I'd never want anyone else to feel.

The following weeks were a nightmare. Julie's face was all over the news. Since she was naming me and Roxy as the murderers, my father was at my neck, asking me why my name was being dragged into it. My parents and Freddy were at my house twenty-four seven, trying to do anything to save the family name.

The first time they asked me if I knew Julie and why she would be accusing me of such a heinous crime, was the following morning. I hadn't yet turned on the TV or looked at the newspaper, so I didn't know what was going on. I couldn't have been happier knowing she was alive. It's a mindfuck to think someone you love so much is dead because of you, and then suddenly finding out they aren't. I was about ready to spill the truth so I could be with her, but the badgering from my parents was what brought me back to the realization that if I admitted it, I would be dead because my father would kill me. So the cycle of not being able to stand up for myself, or the person I loved, continued.

"She's alive?" I asked with this blissful excitement, only to be unmatched by my father's devilish accusation.

"You know this girl, Dalton?" You could hear the distaste he had for me underlying his tone.

"I know a lot of people," I shrugged. "Maybe I've met her before." I can't believe that's how I responded when I should have shouted, 'I'M IN LOVE WITH HER AND YOU NEED TO DO WHATEVER YOU CAN TO HELP HER DAD!

PLEASE! HELP HER!' But I know him, and I knew he wouldn't have. Besides, the truth would have been brought forward that I *was* a part of it. Hearing him call me an idiot or what I've been calling myself, a coward, was something I couldn't bear. Karma's kind of funny that way. I was so fucking terrified of my dad finding out it was because of me that the Blake family name was being tarnished by not going along with Roxy's plan, but in the end, he knew it was me anyways.

"She's obviously mistaken. Right, Dalton?" My mother, always believing no one was better than us. "This is ridiculous! She's just trying to get our money." Yes, and only caring about money. If my dad didn't have any, I probably would have never been born.

"God dammit, Dalton. Look what your little escapades got us into. Freddy has to get on this immediately." It would be easy for him; he was the man who got us out of everything.

I wanted to go and see Julie, but I knew it wouldn't be a good idea for myself in two ways. The first, it would discredit me and the second, I was afraid to face her.

When my day in court rolled around, I felt completely guilty, and not just because I knew the truth. I knew I should have spoken up. I should have admitted I was a part of it and Roxy was the mastermind behind it all, but I didn't. Again, I couldn't. I felt guilty about letting Julie down. I don't know what was wrong with me. God, I hate myself for letting the *one* good thing in my life get away. But that's the thing about life, we have to live with the decisions we make, and I'll be living with the worst one for the rest of my mine.

Chapter 27
Julie 2023

His eyes shot open, panic gracing his face, unsure if I meant what I said. He still thought I was the naive girl, unaware of how the world actually worked. I knew he didn't think I was capable of killing someone, let alone . . . him. But a new Julie was born the day I was given my freedom from the hell I was in. I woke up and realized I had a choice of my own. I could stay the shy, naive Julie I was my entire life or I could take a page out of Roxy's handbook and be someone who didn't take no for an answer. Someone who would always do things for myself when I wanted to and *how* I wanted to. I would make my future what I wanted it to be and I would become someone I always dreamed of becoming. Confident. Powerful. Unstoppable. I would become a new Julie. A stronger Julie. A Julie who wouldn't let anyone hurt her ever again.

As I stared down at Dalton, everything I had felt for him in the past flashed before my eyes like a distant memory. The air around us felt still, and the world seemed to have fallen silent. Even my beloved palm trees didn't move.

"You know I can't do this," he said just above a whisper.

The low growl of his once seductive voice filled the space that held his decision.

"It's not that hard, Dalton. The outcome in either choice will be the same. It's the path to get there that'll be different."

He smirked through his faint cry, not looking at all like the man I thought he once was. "I never thought it would come down to this," he said, reaching for the gun. "You, of all people, Julie." He looked up at me. "I never thought you of all people would end up to be just like her, but who am I kidding? I think we all are, in some fucked up way."

His hand started to tremble as he pulled the gun closer to his face, examining it, feeling the weight in his hands. He laughed, sucking in a tear.

"Why are you making that face?" I asked.

He took a deep breath in, letting it out slowly through his quivering jaw. "I keep telling myself I can do it, but only because it'll make you happy. But . . . " His lower lip began to shake harder. "I can't. I can't do it, Julie. What you're asking me to do is *insane* and doesn't make you any better than her, or me," he paused. "I can't. I can't do it."

"Once a coward, always a coward." I yanked the gun from his hand and walked to his backside. As much as I thought I had changed, I couldn't get myself to see his face for the last time with me being the one to put a bullet through it.

I could hear his silent whimpers as he knelt there, waiting for his end. "Don't do this, Julie. Please!" he cried.

I took a deep breath and cocked the gun. "Now you know what it feels like."

I was taking slow, steady breaths. In through my nose, out through my mouth. My finger on the trigger, slowly beginning to pull when, "I love you, Julie."

And then it ended.

Chapter 28
Dalton 1997

"I guess I'll start by asking you the same question I asked Julie a few years back. What do you think about all this?"

"Well, I never thought I'd ever be in prison, if that's what you mean. Not because I thought I'd get away with being a part of a crime, but . . . . . . *ever*. I never thought I'd be here. I think a lot of people feel that way. But if you're referring to everything I just told you, well, it makes me look pretty stupid and not like the man people thought I was. I look *exactly* like the man my father knew I was though. I didn't do anything to help her. I didn't do anything to save her. Her life could have been everything she hoped it to be, but because of me, and my inability to stand up to my father, to Roxy, too . . . me, I now have to live with the fact that I completely ruined a beautiful woman's life because I was too afraid to upset my dad. In the grand scheme of it all, if I would have known my father would get prison time and I would have been completely unscathed by that, I would have turned Roxy in immediately. I would have told *her* father what she wanted to do and maybe he would have been able to get her the help

"

she truly needed. Most importantly, I would have warned Morgan and maybe she'd still be here today. I know I would have ended up with Julie. I know that much. We'd have that life she talked about. We would be a happy family, something we both longed for, and we'd live out our days growing old together. Just two people in love. But, I obviously didn't see that as a possibility then."

"So, when you found out about Roxy, and the note, how did you feel?"

"Honestly? Relieved."

"How so?"

"I wouldn't have to live with this huge secret hanging over my head anymore. Even though it wouldn't matter to her, I would finally be paying the price for not stopping it in the first place. Julie would be able to live her life again even if it would never actually be the same. She still had a chance. But again, it wasn't because of me. It was because of Roxy."

"So, what do you do in here? How do you pass the time?"

"I write, mostly. I even put money on some guy's books in exchange for teaching me how to play the guitar. I'm actually pretty good. He also helps me put music to the songs I've written."

"What do you write about?"

"Do you really need to ask?"

"I guess not, but it'd be nice to hear it from you directly."

"I'll always write about her, because I'll always be thinking about her. People like Julie don't just appear in your life for no reason."

"And what's the reason you think she came into yours?"

"To show me that I did matter; that I could be loved. Julie showed me that I wanted more out of life than what I thought was ahead of me. She's the only girl I've ever fallen in love with, the only girl I've actually said those words too even if she never heard me say them. I know I messed up, I know I was a coward, and I know that even by some miracle, if I get out of here and see her again, she'll never forgive me. But I'll be damned if I don't spend the rest of my life trying to make it up to her."

Chapter 29
Julie 2023

"What happened? Did you do it? Did you kill him? Julie . . . Julie, why? What . . . why are you laughing?"

"Oh my god! You should have seen your face."

"What? Why is this funny? This isn't funny at all, Julie. What happened to Dalton? What did you do? Did you kill him?

"Well, have you heard anything about him over the years?"

"Julie."

"I'm just kidding. Who do you think I am? Roxy? I really had you going there."

"Julie."

"You have to find humor in this. That's the only way to be okay with everything that happened."

"Are you okay though?"

"Of course I am! And I *do* know what happened. To him after, I mean."

"Umm, let me just refocus here. I just . . . I'm . . . "

"Here let me help you out, I did just throw you for a loop there. Umm, you never forget your first love. So, of course I've thought about him over the years. I *think* about him. Not as much as in the beginning, but over the years, he's popped into my mind."

"Is he still 'that type of guy?' then?"

"He'll *always* be that guy."

"So, do you know what *really* happened to him?"

"Little bits and pieces. I know he served some time for his involvement, but his family had a good team of lawyers, and he got out after four years. I also heard that his mother ran off to Europe out of embarrassment. His father is in prison for malpractice. And from a close source, I heard he moved out of L.A. and changed his name."

"That sounds familiar."

"What does?"

"The leaving L.A. and changing his name part."

"Well, there's more to our story than I told you all those years ago.

"Like what?"

"We were always more connected than what people thought. He'll always be the love of my life."

"Wow! That's a bold statement."

"It's the truth. There's never going to be anyone else like Dalton Blake. No one. He was that person in my life who was meant to be there. We were meant to be together. We had a rare type of love that not everyone gets to experience. We just had the unfortunate circumstances that didn't let us live the life we were supposed to live together."

"How does your partner now . . . . . . is he your husband? Boyfriend?"

"He's my husband."

"Does he know any of this about Dalton? How you feel, I mean?"

"I told him how I felt about him, yes. He understands. He's a really incredible man."

"How did you two meet?"

"He was new to town some odd years after I moved here. I initially didn't take an interest in him. I avoided him because I wasn't wanting anything. One night when I was out at a local bar, he caught my attention when he picked up a guitar and started to play the most beautiful song I'd ever heard. So, I finally mustered up the courage to go up and talk to him. He said that he'd written the song about a girl he once loved and had only learned to play the guitar a few years prior so he could hopefully play it for her one day to win her back. I was impressed, but I played hard to get. My heart was fragile. Then after a few months, I couldn't deny my heart any longer from what it wanted. From what it deserved. To love. Not just to love, but to be loved in a way I thought I was once going to get."

"What's his name?"

"I don't want to put it out there. I don't want people to know who I am. You never know these days with social media."

"I get that. I know you stay off of it."

"Yeah, we're very much private people. We have our local friends, obviously, and Jeffrey and Dawson, who initially didn't like him at first. Other than those select few, we're all each other has."

"He doesn't have any family?"

"I'm his family."

"Why didn't Jeffrey and Dawson like him at first? Were they just being protective of you? What changed?"

"You really want to know every nook and cranny of my life, huh?"

"I'm just curious. I want to know, as I'm sure everyone who followed your story does. We want to know that you're happy and that you have everything you ever wanted."

"That's nice. Well, like you said, they wanted to protect me. They didn't want me to fall for someone who would hurt me again. Someone who they didn't trust. It took a while, but he eventually proved to them that he wouldn't ever frame me for murder."

"Really?!"

"Come on, you have to laugh at that."

"Yeah, I guess so."

"He told them that he once lived a very different life, where he'd been in love with a girl who he never protected, and he let her get away before he even had the chance to tell her how he felt. He then vowed to himself that he would never let that happen again, but if he ever had the chance to make it up to her, he would."

"It sounds like you both have that in common."

"What exactly?"

"Being in love with someone else."

"If that's what you think."

"So, if you ever did see Dalton again, what would you do? Would you forgive him?"

"I think . . . umm . . . I think some people are worth forgiving."

"Even after what he did to you? Going along with Roxy's plan to murder someone and frame you for it? Not to mention, everything in between and not doing a single thing to stop it? You'd still forgive him?"

"Well . . . I know he'd be making it up to me for the rest of his life."

The End

Acknowledgments

To my husband, thank you for believing in me and finally reading my books! I love you!

To my children, here's another accomplishment to add to the list of things you can be proud of your Mom for. I'll always strive to be the cool Mom, even if there may come a time when you won't think so.

Thank you to my editor, Emi Janisch, for being the coolest person and continuing to work with me! Cheers to book three and many more to come!

Felica Hunt, this book was written because of you. Thank you for asking what happened to Julie afterward and sparking the idea that brought this story to life when I thought it was finished.

To my readers, I love and appreciate you more than you will ever know. Being an Indie Author at the beginning of my career has been so rewarding and has formed my friendships with all of you. I want to keep doing this for the rest of my life, and because of your support, I can pursue my wildest dreams. Thank you from the bottom of my heart.

Stay tuned because I have a lot more coming! Please review and spread the word on these little books of mine!

About the Author

Brittany Roth is the author of the beloved Hollywood Psycho trilogy, in which the people you care about most cannot be trusted. In her personal life, she is fortunate not to have that problem. Residing in Southern California with her husband, two kids, and three dogs, she is surrounded by the people—and pets—who love her dearly and would pretty much do anything for her just as she would do anything for them.

When she isn't writing or editing, Brittany can often be found with her closest companion who is always there for her no matter what . . . . . . laundry. No matter how often she's tried to get rid of this acquaintance, it always seems to come back within five seconds of being gone. Who knows, maybe one day there will be a tale of this long-standing unwanted companionship?! Until then, let's just all enjoy the stories she's putting out now, and be grateful she hasn't completely lost her mind yet.